D1249011

The More the Merrier

(A Beany Malone Story)

Lenora Mattingly Weber

The More
The Merrier

THOMAS Y. CROWELL COMPANY
New York

To a reader I am fond of,
Pamela Geyer

1

TODAY was the eleventh of June and a day of departures and good-bys in the Malone household. It was the day after school was out and the first really hot day of summer.

If only there weren't so much hubbub and packing. If only everyone weren't so busy and distracted. For Beany Malone, who was not going anywhere, had plans for her own stay-at-home summer—she had thought of them in bed last night—and she wanted to tell her family about them.

In the big kitchen, she took a pan of cupcakes out of the oven. Upstairs her sister Mary Fred was getting ready for her trip to the dude ranch where she would be working all summer. The luggage in the hall belonged to her father and her pretty stepmother. It was waiting to be packed into the yellow convertible, which would take them to Mexico where her father, Martie Malone, had a newspaper assignment. She mustn't forget to make coffee for them to take in a thermos.

Beany had been trying this whole cluttered day to tell someone of her plans. But they were the kind you had to sort of lead up to. You couldn't just blurt them out, or the one you blurted them out to would be sure to say, "Beany! You must be off your rocker!"

She walked through the hall and called to Mary Fred upstairs. But Mary Fred was in the bathroom with the water running and couldn't hear.

Her father had taken the car to get it checked; her stepmother, Adair, was up at the five-and-ten for something they would need on the trip. Even Beany's brother Johnny was across the street, sprinkling the lawn of a neighbor who had also gone on a trip. Beany was just thinking of going across the street to talk over her project with him, when Mary Fred called down the stairs, "Hey, Beany, I can't get everything in the suitcase."

Here was Beany's chance.

In her upstairs room Mary Fred was throwing jodhpur breeches, suntan lotion, a square-dance dress, riding boots, and frilly bouffant petticoats into a suitcase in her usual blithe, haphazard manner. "Give me a hand, hon," she said.

Mary Fred was the eldest of the Malone children at home since Elizabeth had married and left. She was twenty and had just finished her sophomore year at the University. Beany would be a senior next year at Harkness High *and* the editor of the school paper, *Hark Ye*. She was still awed by and uneasy about the honor; all the more uneasy, because she would be following in the footsteps of Jennifer Reed, outgoing editor.

2

Beany had an instant mental picture of Jennifer Reed with her dark, close-cropped hair and ivory skin. Jennifer was so poised, so competent, so unruffled. Beany also had an instant mental picture of Jennifer's home in that exclusive district east of the University, called Harmony Heights. It took words like *spacious, de luxe, well-kept, gracious* to describe it. So like a picture out of one of those beautiful-homes magazines. It was certainly a far cry from the big, scuffed, two-story Malone home.

The two sisters, Beany and Mary Fred, looked alike. They both had grayish blue eyes under dark brows and lashes. Yet there were times when Beany felt that Mary Fred had got the best of it when looks and personality were handed out. Mary Fred's hair was darker than Beany's and had a natural curl. Beany's hair had darkened from the straw color it had been in childhood; nowadays her brother Johnny addressed her, "Hey, you with the roan braids—" Beany wore her two stubby braids pinned across her head. But she had reached the point where it would take only a small push to make her enter a beauty shop and say, "I've decided to have my braids cut off."

Mary Fred had no freckles. Certainly that splash of freckles across her own nose and cheeks was not a girl's best friend, Beany had decided long ago. But the most enviable thing about Mary Fred was that gay and happy confidence in herself and the world. Johnny always called her "old bubble and bounce." Beany was slower to bubble, slower to bounce.

She busied herself, repacking Mary Fred's suitcase, though even she doubted if she could find room for the jodhpur boots, and said, "I told you, didn't I, that I was

3

elected editor-in-chief of *Hark Ye* for next year?" This was leading up to Beany's secret.

"Not more than six times," Mary Fred answered from the closet. "I thought I had another white blouse."

Beany swallowed down the sisterly insult about the six times. "What worries me is following Jennifer Reed. Whenever the staff needed to get together, she called meetings at her house. She had a special room in the basement. I wish you could see it, Mary Fred. Cherry red carpeting from wall to wall. And rattan tub chairs with cushions of yellow and green and black. It was so right, that room. No wonder Jennifer can be such a marvelous hostess."

"The hostess with the mostess, eh!" Mary Fred squinted at the nylon stockings she was holding up to the light. "If the run isn't too wide, I can turn it on the inside and trust it won't show . . . I thought Jennifer was going to have an outgoing-Jennifer, incoming-Beany party? That's an old Harkness High tradition."

"She is," Beany said. "She couldn't give it before school closed because they sold their house. So she's having to stretch tradition a bit and give it when they're moved and settled."

Mary Fred peered anxiously out the window. "I wish the boy friend would arrive. He knows we have to allow for loading up a mare and colt in a trailer and making slower time to the ranch."

Beany tried another approach to telling Mary Fred the plans that had kept her awake for hours the night before. "Mary Fred, you know how I like to cook—"

"Comes as natural to you as kicking to a cow," Mary Fred said promptly, "which is more than can be said of that bewitching Mary Fred Malone."

4

Beany hurried on earnestly, "When we took turns cooking for the family, I kept track of what it *actually* cost to feed a person for a month. Dormitory board is over thirty dollars more than what it costs. And I remember you and the other girls saying it wasn't very good, and so I thought—"

"Rice!" Mary Fred snorted. "Macaroni! I never had lunch with the gals at the dorm that they didn't have rice or macaroni for waddin'. . . . Look, hon, swap me that white blouse you've got on for this candy-striped one." Mary Fred was peeling off her blouse. "Stripes look gruesome with my red riding jacket."

Beany took off her white blouse and handed it to Mary Fred. She was getting the worst of the bargain, for the candy-striped one was faded and two of the pearl buttons had been replaced by ones that didn't match. But she couldn't take time to haggle. Even as she buttoned it, she glanced about the two-room suite Mary Fred was leaving. One room was a study or sitting room, the other a glassed-in porch with two beds. "You see, Mary Fred, here are these two rooms of yours and these two beds that'll just be going to waste when you're gone, and so I thought—"

Mary Fred wasn't even listening. "I tell you! I'll *wear* my jodhpur boots, and then you can squeeze these loafers in." She added as she pushed her feet into the boots and stamped each one on snugly, "Gosh, toots, I hate to think of you and Johnny rattling around in this big, empty house. Why don't the two of you come up to the Lazy J for a few days? I could even ask the boss to give you a rate."

Beany said vehemently, "That's what I'm trying to tell you. I won't be rattling around in this big, empty house.

5

I'm going to make money. Because when I'm editor of *Hark Ye,* I'll have to have meetings here. The meetings at Jennifer's were always private. And can you imagine anything private in the Malone house? Can't you just imagine Johnny barging in on us and telling us how to get the paper out, and thinking he's a treat?"

"He usually is," Mary Fred defended.

Part of Beany's mind had to concede that Johnny, the warmhearted and gifted, was a treat. But she went on heatedly, "And you know how Dad always has newspaper people around—usually crackpots—and how Adair has to use the living room or dining room for her easel and her pictures—"

Adair, the Malone stepmother, was a portrait painter.

"Poor old Adair," Mary Fred murmured. "It's just a shame she doesn't have a room of her own for a studio so she wouldn't have to paint all over the house."

Beany flung out, "What about poor old Beany? Here, I'm following Jennifer as a hostess—"

A car horn honked in the Malone driveway.

"At long last, my man!" Mary Fred said in relief. She had only time to say, "Does this wonderful Jennifer know she's your idol?"

Beany flushed but didn't answer. Mary Fred didn't have to put it so bluntly.

Mary Fred added, "Don't get bitter, chum, because you can't be another Jennifer Reed. The only daughter of the big Christopher Reed Realty Company is many thousands of dollars removed from Beany Malone. And, after all, everybody likes to come to the Malones. . . . You carry down the suitcase and I'll struggle with the loose stuff. We got any apples?"

"Apples?"

6

"For the passenger in the trailer. Miss Goldie is a nursing mother and needs refreshment en route."

Beany found the apples. She told Mary Fred good-by. . . . Don't get bitter. You couldn't help turning a little bitter when Mary Fred was more concerned about a mare and colt than with the plans and dreams of her own sister.

No sooner was Mary Fred gone than the loading of the yellow convertible started. "Make it iced coffee, Beany," her father called. "It's going to be a hot drive."

Back in the kitchen Beany poured coffee into the wide mouth of a thermos jug and dropped in ice cubes. Two cubes too many plopped out of the ice tray and into the full jug, splashing coffee onto the table and Beany.

She sopped it up and reached for the cap of the thermos. She had to step over and around the long legs of her brother Johnny, who was sitting sidewise on the floor, looking through the catch-all bottom drawer of the cupboard.

"Do tell!" he muttered in triumph. "I can't find that extra cup for the thermos, but look—the sunglasses for Dad we've been looking for all day."

He stood up and blew noisy breaths on the dark glasses and wiped them on the tail of his white T shirt. He was nineteen, and two years older and a head taller than his youngest sister. "That's life for you, Beany. You look for one thing and don't find it, but you find something else that's more important."

Beany gave his philosophy little thought. Maybe she could tell him about the plans that were yeasting inside her.

"Johnny, when Dad and Adair leave, you and I will be here all alone on our own."

"We've been on our own before," he said cheerfully.

7

That was true, of course. Their father was a columnist on the morning paper, the *Call*. Wherever there were stories of public interest, there went Martie Malone and his portable typewriter. In the six years between the death of their mother and the acquiring of Adair for a stepmother, the young Malones had indeed often been on their own. Johnny always referred to Martie Malone as "our off-again, on-again, gone-again father."

"Well, don't you think it'd be sort of silly to let all those beds—the two in Mary Fred's room and the big double bed in Dad's and Adair's room—go to waste?" Beany said by way of introducing her still-secret plans.

"Oh, they probably won't go to waste long. You know how people are always dropping in at the Malones'." He was trying on the dark glasses. "Hm'm, a spot of gravy that spit won't take off." He walked to the sink and said, over the sound of running water, "Hey, Beaver, hand me one of those paper napkins."

Beany's father was at the front door, calling with a man's impatience, "Adair, aren't you ready? Let's get going. Beany, how about the coffee?"

She hurried out to the packed car with it. She said, "Dad, you know that big old wine room in the basement?"

He chuckled, "That hasn't seen a bottle of wine in twenty-five years."

Adair, Beany's young stepmother, came out with an unfinished canvas, which she wedged into the car. The pockets of her green skirt bulged with tubes of paint and paint brushes.

Beany pursued, "Is it all right, Dad, if I make the wine room into sort of a rumpus room this summer so I can—"

8

"A rumpus room? Good grief, honey, we've already got nine rooms in the house and every one is a rumpus room."

"That's just it," Beany said. "I want a private rumpus room to get away from all the public rumpus."

Johnny loped out with the dark glasses and his father said, "Oh, good!" and put them on.

"Of course it'll take money to fix up the old wine room, but I was thinking in the night—"

"My typewriter!" Martie Malone exclaimed suddenly. "I knew I was forgetting something. Here I'm going down to Mexico to do profiles of the most important men of their country, and I darn near forgot my typewriter. Bring it out, Johnny."

As he packed it in, he had to sidestep the big Irish setter who watched his every move with desolate eyes. He stopped to pat the dog and say, "No, Red, you can't go. You stay home and look after Beany and Johnny. . . . That everything, Adair? Let's shove off."

Wouldn't anyone listen to Beany Malone? Wasn't anyone interested in her summer?

Evidently not. Her stepmother, with her close-cut auburn curls, was taking smeary tubes of paint out of her skirt pockets and crowding them into the glove compartment, and saying, "I hate to run out on you kids like this. I hope you won't have a lonely summer."

"We won't," Beany said, her square jaw setting stubbornly.

"Don't give us a thought, Adair," Johnny said. "Just look after the old man."

Beany's father kissed her good-by; all the parental advice had already been given. "We'll keep in touch with you," he said, starting the motor. "If you need any help or advice—or money, there's always Judge Buell next door."

And then the laden convertible was driving out between the wide gateposts, leaving Beany and Johnny alone in the side yard. Johnny pushed back his dark thatch of hair and grinned ruefully. "Does give you a kind of Last of the Mohicans feeling, doesn't it?" he said and bent down to comfort the dog.

He reached out for Beany's wrist to look at her watch. "Oops, I didn't know it was so late. I have to leg it out to the campus library and look up some colorful data on old-time gamblers for my prof."

During the school year, Johnny earned his tuition at the University by doing research for his history professor. During the summer, the professor gave a Friday night TV program on the early days of Colorado and Denver. Johnny helped him find material for it, too. If there was one thing Johnny knew it was the settling of the West. Sometimes it seemed to Beany that those long-dead pioneers and buffalo hunters were more real to him than the people he saw every day.

As he turned toward the gate, Beany laid a detaining hand on his arm. "Wait, Johnny. I've got to show you something. I've got to tell you something."

"Tell me later, Beaver." He shook off her hold. "I have to dig up something on old Soapy Smith who used to wrap a ten-dollar bill inside the wrapper of a bar of soap, and then hawk the soap and—need I say?—no one ever found the bill in his bar of soap."

"But, Johnny, this is important."

"So is this important. It's my job, remember? And I've got a car to make payments on, remember?"

10

Beany dropped down on the porch step. A fine thing. A fine thing. Mary Fred, so engrossed in Miss Goldie and her colt she wouldn't even listen. Her father, with no thought for anyone but those important men in Mexico he would be writing "profiles" of. And now Johnny, so carried away by some old rapscallion named Soapy Smith that he couldn't take time to listen to his own sister's beautiful plans for the summer. It was enough to make any girl bitter.

Red nuzzled at her knees. Maybe it would ease the pressure inside her to confide in Red, even though he couldn't answer back.

And then even Red left her to run in tail-wagging welcome to the gate. Beany looked up at the visitor who was coming through it. He was a giant of a man in clerical black, with broad shoulders and thick graying hair that seemed to push his black hat up on his head. His face over the Roman collar was ruddy and knobby, and his bushy eyebrows stuck up in untidy tufts that gave his face a roguish and quizzical look.

Beany took a step to meet him. "Father Hugh!" she said, and reached out her hand to be grasped in his big firm one.

Father Hugh O'Higgins was an old friend of the Malones. "A holy man and a fighting Irishman," Martie Malone called him. His parish was in Twin Pine, thirteen miles away in the foothills. And he helped at a downtown mission in Denver, aiding the poor and unfortunate. "Here's Father Hugh," Martie Malone used to call out to the family when the priest stepped into the house. "So lock the icebox and guard your extra pair of shoes. He's got his begging look."

The times, the times, Father Hugh had interrupted a

11

conversation to say, "By the way, you don't happen to have a sweater that'd fit a lad of twelve, do you?" Or, "You wouldn't have an extra cooking kettle, would you? There's a poor soul down at the Mission—"

He folded Beany's hand in his two big ones. "Did all the travelers get off?" There was a burr of Irish brogue in his voice. "And are you here alone and feeling like the girl they left behind in this big empty house?"

Beany held tight to his hands, fearing, somehow, that if she didn't he, too, would go hurrying off. She had to tell someone. She drew a long breath, said, "The house won't be empty for long, Father Hugh. I'm going to keep boarders this summer."

2

THE priest did not look surprised. Or perhaps he was used to people blurting out even more startling things than that. He didn't say, "Beany! You must be off your rocker," but "Are you, now? What for?"

"Come with me, Father Hugh, and I'll show you what for."

He followed her obediently into the house, murmuring as he crossed the threshold, "God bless this house."

Beany led the way down to the basement. To the left was the workaday part with its laundry tubs, drying racks, and water heater. Beyond that was the furnace room. To the right was the seldom used door which opened into what they still called the wine room though, as Beany's father said, it was like the butler's pantry upstairs in which no butler ever set foot.

Beany shoved open the creaking door. Her explanation

tumbled out, "I'm going to make this into a sort of private rumpus room. I lay awake the longest time last night planning it. Next year I'm to be editor of our school paper, and I want a place where we can hold staff meetings. This last year we went to Jennifer Reed's, and she had the loveliest room—"

She paused for breath. She wished Father Hugh would say something, instead of staring at the dank and musty room. He didn't step inside. And Red, who had followed them down, only stood outside the door, sniffing dubiously.

Beany herself felt a little daunted. Somehow it had been easier to visualize the finished perfection of the room last night when she had lain awake in her bed. She hadn't remembered how rough and uneven those brick walls were; she had pictured those two windows as being deeper—

She began talking even faster to recapture her dream. "I'll do two of the walls in oyster white and two in forest green. And have red wall-to-wall carpeting to cover up the cement floor. Jennifer had tub chairs and these sectional couches. We've got an old studio couch up in the attic I can cover in chartreuse." At the blank look on Father Hugh's face, she added, "Don't you think chartreuse would be pretty?"

"Chartreuse? Ah yes, that's a yellow that turned green with envy."

Beany motioned to the dingy light bulb that hung on a cord from the ceiling. "I think Johnny could take that out and put in one that looks like a lantern. And I'll buy about twelve tub chairs with bright seat pads to go with them. I'll have to figure on seating fourteen or fifteen."

14

"Now why are you figuring on bringing your company down here when you've all that room upstairs?"

Again Beany drew a long breath. "It was always private at Jennifer Reed's. And you know how it is here. Can you imagine us, trying to hold a meeting upstairs with the phone ringing, and Mary Fred and her dates all over the place, and Dad having newspaper people, and Johnny barging in? And sometimes Adair has a picture on an easel that she's working on, and even Red here keeps nuzzling up to everyone just to be patted—"

"How old are you, child?"

"I was seventeen on St. Patrick's Day."

He nodded soberly, though his deepset eyes twinkled. "It came to me at sixteen—that craving for privacy and wishing I were an orphan. So you're going to keep boarders to make the money for all the fancy fixing-up down here. But don't you have a job at helping this woman that writes the Advice to the Lovelorn column in the *Call*?"

"No, Eve Baxter took the summer off because her eyes were bothering her. That's one reason I want to keep boarders to make money. I noticed cherry red carpeting in a store up on the boulevard—um-mm, it's luscious."

"How many boarders are you going to keep?"

"Four. Two in Mary Fred's room, and two in Dad's and Adair's. That would only be six to cook for, counting Johnny and me. All winter long Mary Fred and I took turns cooking for the family—and there are five of us—and we went to school besides. I can clear over thirty dollars per head each month if I charge summer-school students what they'd have to pay at the dorm. What really decided me," Beany went on, wishing Father Hugh showed more enthusiasm, "was a notice in the Varsity paper Johnny brought home. It said that Brent Hall

15

wouldn't be able to accommodate all the summer students and anyone who could provide board please to register at the Housing Office."

The doubtful look on the priest's face was replaced by a smile. "You were always a great hand at cooking. I remember coming to the Malones' when you were no higher than the stove, and eating your doughnuts."

"I was twelve," she said. "I was taking cooking in junior high, and then I tried out all the recipes at home." Beany's mind flicked back to those years after her mother's death. Housekeepers had come and gone; if Beany hadn't been a great hand at cooking, it would often have been skimpy fare for the young Malones. She murmured, "I like to cook. I like feeding people."

"Bless you," he said. "I can't think of a happier home for these out-of-town students than here with you and Johnny."

Beany glowed inwardly. Now she felt better. At last she had shared her secret and his "Bless you," was like someone saying, "Of course you can do it."

"Goodness, Father Hugh, I didn't even offer you a cup of coffee."

"Not today, Beany. I must be getting home. I left my car at the garage to have the clutch fixed, so I'll have to take a bus back to Twin Pine. If your father were home, I'd talk him into driving me back."

"I can drive you to Twin Pine in Johnny's car," she offered. "He's out at the campus library, probing into the life of Soapy Smith."

"Do you suppose the baling wire he's got it patched up with will hold together long enough?"

Beany laughed. "That's an insult, Father Hugh. This

is a newer old car. Johnny traded in his puddle-jumper on it; and he gave it a new paint job—light blue with black fenders; and he calls it Blue Monday, because the first Monday of every month he has to make a payment on it."

She was getting the car keys when Father Hugh said, "By the way, Beany, would you happen to have an extra blanket? There's a poor family moved into Twin Pine with a lot of little ones, and you know how cold the nights are in the hills."

She found an extra blanket, a shawl, and a wool dress of her own she had outgrown.

And so Beany, behind the wheel of Johnny's little car, set out with him to his parish at Twin Pine, thirteen miles out of the city.

Sitting beside him, she bubbled over with her plans. "At first, it looked as though the whole summer would be so empty. Because everybody was leaving town for the summer—not only family, but all my friends. My girl friend, Miggs Carmody, the one who was keeping the mare and colt for Mary Fred, went to British Columbia with her folks. But the boss at the dude ranch is letting her keep them there for the summer."

"How about your boy friends? I hope the Beany Malone heart department isn't empty."

"I'm the girl that was left behind there, too. Hank, the School of Mines senior that I had dates with, has gone off on a geological survey for the summer. And then of course, Andy's in the Marines."

She couldn't think of Andy Kern without a wave of nostalgia. Life had its own exciting pickup when Andy was around. She missed his crinkly grin, his calling her

17

knucklehead, or pie-face, or doll. But Andy had joined the Marines last March. He had already been home on leave after boot training. It was time for her to be sending him another box of cookies.

"But that's all right," Beany said staunchly, "if I'm left to wither on the vine. Because this whole summer I'm just going to be a mercenary landlady and think only dollar-thoughts."

"Are you now?" he said. It was strange the meaning he could put into those three words. It was almost as though he said, "That, I've got to see—Beany Malone only thinking dollar-thoughts a whole summer long."

She slowed to take a detour because of road construction. A workman was setting in place the black iron pots, the flares that would be lighted as soon as it was dark to guide motorists to the detour.

The sun was sinking behind the mountains as Beany stopped in front of the stone rectory beside the stone church. Father Hugh said he wouldn't ask her in, because he wanted her to get home before dark. He thanked her for the ride, and promised he'd catch her a mess of trout the very first chance he got. "Go with God," he said in parting, and turned back to add, "Don't drive too fast."

Beany hummed happily on the way back, as the car rattled over the rutted and dusty detour. She turned onto her own Barberry Street. Lights were already lighted in houses, and there was Red waiting at the curb for someone in the family to return. On the Malone side of the street, which faced west, just three large two-story houses with wide lawns took up the block. Across the street the houses were newer one-story ones, crowded closer together.

18

As Beany stopped the car, her eyes were caught by the stout figure of a woman slumped down beside a suitcase on the top step of the house across the street. Who would be sitting on the Fletcher front steps with the house unlighted and locked behind her? Mrs. Fletcher had gone to visit her married daughter in Oregon. She had come to the Malones two days ago to arrange with Johnny to care for her lawn during her absence.

Beany climbed out of the car. The woman on the steps got up and started toward her. They met on the curbing in front of the Fletcher house. Beany drew a surprised breath. It wasn't a woman at all. It was a very plump girl about Beany's age, with a round, childish face that looked tired and anxious.

She burst out, "Do you know anything about Mrs. Fletcher? I'm Lisa Hold, and she's my cousin Josie—that is, Dad's cousin Josie. I came on the bus from Wichita, and she isn't home. The man next door said he thought she was out of town. But he said he and his wife both worked, and maybe you folks across the street would know, because he said he saw the Malone boy watering the lawn—"

"Yes, Johnny's taking care of it. He's my brother. I'm Beany Malone. Mrs. Fletcher went to visit her daughter in Oregon. I guess she decided kind of suddenly to go, because her daughter's going to have a baby."

"Oh, mercy!" the girl breathed. "I never thought about her going to Oregon—I didn't think Martha was going to have her baby till August. I just kept hoping maybe she was downtown shopping, and so I kept waiting—"

"Well, for goodness' sake," a puzzled Beany said. "If she knew you were coming, why didn't she let you know she wouldn't be here?"

"I—I decided to come all at once—and I never thought about her not being home." She added defensively, "I used to see her when she'd come to visit Grandma, and she was always saying, 'I want you to come and visit me in Denver sometime. It's lonely since Martha left.' I don't know what to do. I'm so tired. I didn't sleep any last night on the bus—and it was late getting in—and then I got lost coming out here. I thought maybe she left a key with you folks. She wouldn't mind if I went in and rested."

Beany shook her head. "Oh no, she's the kind that bolts and bars the place if she just goes out to lunch. Gee, I shouldn't think your folks would let you start out without being sure she'd be at the bus station to meet you."

Lisa Hold from Wichita didn't answer. Beany saw that it was all she could do to keep from crying. Oh-oh, she must have had a row with her folks, and that's why she'd left on such short notice. But she looked so woebegone and weary and, in spite of her size, so young and defenseless. Beany felt a sharp stab of pity. She couldn't just walk off and leave her and her suitcase in front of a locked house.

She said, "Well, Lisa, you'd better come on home with me. We're just across the street. There's no one home but Johnny and me, so you could even stay all night and then take a bus back to Wichita tomorrow."

Lisa managed to choke out, "That's awfully nice of you."

Between them they carried the suitcase across the street. The red setter escorted them through the Malone gate and up the porch steps and through the front door. "Just put the suitcase here in the hall," Beany said, "and come on out in the kitchen while I fix us something to eat."

20

3

IN the lighted kitchen Lisa Hold looked even heavier than she had in the dusk outside. Goodness, that double chin! And goodness, that bulgy old-lady blouse! It was made of a durable gray-striped material. Maybe someone had told her that stripes were "thinning." There was hardly a waistline where the striped blouse and dark gathered skirt met. She didn't need any crinoline petticoat to hold out the skirt; it was all girl under it.

Beany cleared off the kitchen table, thinking: But she'd be pretty if she weren't so fat. If her face weren't so round, her eyes and lips wouldn't look so swallowed up. Her eyes are that violet blue, and her skin does have that "petal of a flower" look. She ought to do something about her hair —it's too long to be short, and too short to be long.

She opened the refrigerator door and asked, "Are you hungry?" and Lisa answered, with a rueful laugh, "I'm

21

always hungry." Beany added, "The phone's there in the hall. Do you want to call the bus station and see about a bus going back to Wichita?"

A wincing pain passed over Lisa's face. Her soft face set in stubborn lines. "I'd die before I went back there where I'm not wanted. They're all so glad I'm gone—now Mom and Jeanie can go merrily on with all the trousseau and parties for Jeanie—"

"Is she your sister? Is she going to get married?"

Lisa nodded to both questions. She gave a poor semblance of a laugh. "And they didn't know what to do with me. They didn't count on having me on their hands this summer."

"What did they do with you other summers?" Beany, the practical, asked.

"I was always with Grandma Hold. She lived in a little town near Wichita, and I always went there when school was out—ever since I was a little girl—" She gave a sheepish, appealing smile. "Only I was never a very *little* girl. The last couple of years I lived with her because Grandma was so heavy and short of breath it was hard for her to get around. She died in April. Cousin Josie came back for the funeral and she said again that she wanted me to come and see her—"

"And did you go home after your grandmother died?"

"Yes, only it didn't seem like home. Jeanie's always been so pretty and popular; and I've always been fat, and scared of people."

The fat ugly duckling with a pretty sister! Beany thought fleetingly of what a field day Mary Fred, the psychology major, would have with poor Lisa. Beany had typed one of Mary Fred's papers that was on overeating as compensation.

Lisa was saying wistfully, "It was so nice at Grandma's. There were just the two of us, and she never nagged at me about being a fat monstrosity."

Beany opened her mouth, about to say, Why don't you reduce, when Lisa said despairingly, "I'm so sick of people telling me to reduce. I can't help being fat. It runs in the family on the Hold side—"

"Is your father heavy, too?"

"No, it happened to skip him. And that's why he can't understand, either." There it was again—that wincing. "But, just as Grandma always said, when it's glandular, there's nothing you can do about it." And then, without warning, her face went slack, and she gulped out, "Jeanie doesn't want me to be her bridesmaid when she gets married this fall. She said I'd turn the whole wedding into a farce—she said I'd be a—a laughingstock." She looked down at her lap, began bunching the striped goods of her skirt between her fingers.

Beany felt an ache in her own throat. Supposing Mary Fred were getting married and wouldn't have *her* for a bridesmaid? She took tomatoes out of the refrigerator, sliced them. She talked, as she worked, trying to divert Lisa's mind. "I hope you don't mind a lot of odds and ends. Oh-oh, I see Johnny's been home, so the best slices of ham are no more."

No answer except the sound of Lisa's swallowing down sobs. Beany talked on. "I'm planning on taking in boarders this summer. With just Johnny and me here in this big house, we've got room for them."

Evidently she had succeeded in diverting her guest from her own woes, for a lumpy voice said, "That'll be nice. How many boarders are you going to have?"

"Four, I hope. I want to make enough money to turn

23

the wine room in the basement into a rumpus room. You see, I'm to be editor of the school paper this coming year, and I follow a girl named Jennifer Reed—and gosh, that's quite an order. About half of the staff have worked under Jennifer this year and have gone to meetings and parties in her rumpus room, and I don't want them to feel it's a comedown when they come here. I'm going to do two of the walls in forest green, and two in oyster white, and then use a lot of red and chartreuse. I just wish the windows weren't so dinky."

Lisa's voice sounded as if she had a stuffy cold, but she said eagerly, "You could make the windows look bigger if you put curtain rods out over the wall, because mostly your meetings will be in the evening, won't they? And you know what would be pretty, and sort of Greenwich Village? You could make the curtains of theatrical gauze, real full, with bands on them of all the colors in the room—red, dark green, and chartreuse. They wouldn't cost much either. I could make them for you. Even if I'm over at Cousin Josie's, I could."

"Thanks," Beany said, with a rush of feeling. Lisa was nice. And it was balm to Beany's soul to have someone enter wholeheartedly into her plans after all the brush-offs from the busy Malones today.

By now Lisa was on her feet and reaching for dishes in the cupboard. Beany said, "We can just eat here in the kitchen."

"Grandma and I always ate in the kitchen too, except for the evenings when we ate in front of TV. My folks in Wichita have one of these little narrow kitchens and I was always bumping into everything. No, I didn't fit in—in more ways than one." She tried to laugh.

Beany slid bread into the toaster, said, "But I still don't

24

see why your folks would let you start out for Denver without knowing that Mrs. Fletcher would be here and meet your bus."

Lisa flushed. "I lied to them," she confessed. "I told them that she wrote and wanted me to come out because she was lonely. I just had to leave. Oh, it was so awful. Mom and Jeanie were so busy shopping, and they'd come home with new clothes, and then they'd give me the old routine about reducing because they didn't want to buy outsize, frumpy clothes for me. And there were all those luncheons and showers for Jean, and there was Fatty, the problem, they didn't know whether to ask or leave out—"

She took a minute to swallow hard, and added in a thin voice, "They were all so relieved when I told them Cousin Josie wanted me to visit her. And that's why I can't go back now. I can just see their faces drop if I should walk in and say, 'Here I am.' I guess I was at Grandma's too long."

"Oh, I don't think their faces would drop," Beany said, but she could see that Lisa was unconvinced.

"Beany, I don't think Cousin Josie will be gone very long. I know whenever she came to visit Grandma she was always edgy about getting back to her flowers and her club and everything. Could I stay with you until she comes home? I can pay you board. I brought out two fifty-dollar government bonds that Grandma bought for me a long time ago."

She rushed on, "You can see, can't you, that I can't go home? If I can't stay here, I don't know where to go."

Beany was filling two glasses with milk. There it was—a warm swelling inside her. Johnny called it her "do-good-ing instinct."

She couldn't stand Lisa's unhappiness without doing

25

something for her. Her lips couldn't possibly have shaped a No. Instead they said, "I don't see why you couldn't stay until Mrs. Fletcher comes back."

Lisa sighed in grateful relief. "I'll help you with the work. Grandma was German and she taught me to cook and clean and wash and iron. I'll help you paint your rumpus room. I've painted her kitchen and bathroom and porches. I can cash the bonds at any bank. I'll pay whatever you say."

Beany said hesitantly, "You can just pay enough for the extra cost of the groceries." After all, you couldn't charge dormitory board to a girl who would be helping with the work. And besides, Lisa would be moving across the street to Mrs. Fletcher's in a couple of weeks at the most.

"Let's eat," Beany said.

Lisa ate hungrily. Beany kept inserting slices of bread in the toaster which Lisa spread thickly with butter and jam. She didn't bother to cut the fat off the slices of ham she reached for. She put more mayonnaise on the tomato and cottage cheese salad. She drank three glasses of milk and ate two cupcakes.

"I made these so Dad and Adair could take some on their trip, but I didn't have time to ice them," Beany said. "Tomorrow I want to make cookies to send to Andy Kern. He's in the Marines at San Diego." She chuckled, "I asked Andy what kind of cookies he liked best, and he wrote back and said 'Lots' and 'Often.'"

For a minute wistful longing clouded Lisa's face. "I never got a letter from a boy," she murmured.

"Haven't you? Didn't you date the boys at school?" Now that was a stupid thing to say. There was a girl at

Harkness High with a lot of extra poundage, and what a wide berth the boys gave her. Now that *would* be something to be bitter about.

Lisa said in a flat voice, "I never went to school parties or dances." She got heavily to her feet, and started picking up dishes. Even though Beany said, "You're so tired, Lisa, why don't you go on to bed?" she worked with Beany until the kitchen was put to rights.

She took Lisa and her suitcase up to Mary Fred's two-room suite. Both the inside room and the sleeping porch were in a state of disorder. "School was just out yesterday," Beany apologized, "and Mary Fred had to scurry around to pack and take off. And she never was the orderly type."

Again Lisa helped her straighten up and pick up.

"There now," Beany said. "Pick out either bed you want and fall in."

Lisa rummaged through her suitcase and produced a gown. It, Beany noted, was a round-necked muslin one. Golly, she and her fat grandmother must have cut their clothes from the same bolt.

Like a tired child, Lisa pulled off her clothes and slid the shapeless gown over her head. Even as Beany finished stacking books and notebooks on the desk in the inside room, Lisa dropped down on Mary Fred's pillow and murmured drowsily, "Beany, you're swell to take me in. I'll make the cookies for you to send to Andy tomorrow."

Beany turned out the light and walked slowly down the stairs. A temporary but nonprofit boarder already. This was a fine start for a dollar-minded landlady.

27

4

BEANY turned on TV and sat watching it absently. She wished Johnny would come home so she could ask him about Mrs. Fletcher's plans, and so she could tell him to go to the Housing Office on the campus the very first thing in the morning and list the Malone boarding house.

When the commercial came on, she got up and fidgeted about the house. Even if Lisa were still here, a summer-school student wouldn't mind sharing Mary Fred's quarters with her, would she? And there would surely be two summer-school males who wouldn't mind sleeping together in the double bed in her parents' room. That wall-to-wall carpeting in her rumpus room called for a staggering outlay.

She went down to the wine room again and tried to gauge how many square yards it would take. She stepped it off. Heavens, it was about fifteen feet long—five yards, and twelve feet wide—four yards. Twenty square yards!

28

She drifted to the kitchen and took down from the cupboard the round oatmeal box in which she always kept the household funds, and which Johnny called Beany's Sinking Fund. Both she and Mary Fred used this simplified system of accounting. They put the money for running the house in the oatmeal box and dipped into it for shopping at the supermarket and paying the milkman. Whatever was left at the end of their housekeeping stint was profit.

Beany took off the lid and peered in at the money that was already there. It was what her father had left her and Johnny to run the house on until the first of July, when he would send more. It was a generous enough allowance so that if she shopped with a shrewd eye for food that was cheap and filling, she could save a considerable amount.

Oh, she knew ways to stretch a budget. Stale bread for French toast. The straggly bits of ham left around the bone for ham timbales. Why couldn't she, too, bear down heavily on rice and macaroni for waddin'?

What was keeping Johnny? She wanted to ask him how soon summer school started.

Three paying boarders, even if Lisa's stay overlapped. Over thirty dollars profit on each. Over ninety dollars per month. Maybe if she got a small eater or two, she could clear even more. Why, supposing the basement room did take twenty yards of carpeting? And let's see, twelve tub chairs at six eighty each; the bright-colored cushions were extra.

She stopped in the dining room and surveyed the long table, visualizing it with boarders around it and Beany Malone at the end behind the coffee pot . . . "Beany, I never ate such delicious meat balls." . . . "Why, these cheese biscuits fairly melt in your mouth." Just one big happy family.

She wished Johnny would come home, so she could ask him how long summer school lasted.

On the desk in the living room she saw a letter she had started to Andy Kern. She couldn't wait to tell him about her ambitious plans. She sat down and wrote:

> Guess what I'm going to do? I'm going to keep boarders, and make enough to furnish a room in our basement like Jennifer Reed's rumpus room.

She unfolded Andy's latest letter and read it over. One part caught her attention.

> I've been buddying around with a ploughboy from Kansas and—wouldn't you know?—everybody calls him Kansas, though his name is Joe Kaswell. Nice guy, but I can't figure anybody being as bashful as he is. He hasn't got a girl. He never had one. He's never had a letter from one.

So Beany added in her letter to Andy,

> I've got a girl who is going to stay here for a while. And she said tonight that *she* never had a letter from a boy.

She hesitated over adding, "But I don't wonder, because she's so fat." No, that didn't seem cricket. So she signed it, "The Landlady at Beany's Boarding House."

Maybe she had better write her parents about her plans for the summer that she hadn't been able to tell them. So she wrote that she had decided to board a few summer school students to make money for—

She stopped. It would be more fun not to tell them what the money was for. And then, when they returned in September, she could take them down the basement steps and throw open the door to the wine room and overwhelm them with the finished room. So she finished the sentence with, "—something I want." She went on to tell about Lisa Hold, a relative of Mrs. Fletcher's, who would be staying with them until Mrs. Fletcher returned.

She would have explained more, but she heard a car in the driveway. Someone was evidently bringing Johnny home. She signed her letter, "Love, Beany," and was sealing it when she heard Johnny's step on the front porch, heard him call back to someone, "I'll take my load right on upstairs. Think you can manage the rest?"

She reached the front hall just as Johnny opened the screen door and came in, carrying coats and shirts on hangers, and a wall lamp. He said, "Grab the lamp, Beany, before I drop it. Guess what? I've brought home a boarder."

"You did! Well, I've already brought one home. She's asleep now up in Mary Fred's room, but she'll only stay until—"

"Didn't I tell you," Johnny interrupted happily, "that those beds just crying to be used wouldn't be crying very long?"

"—just till Mrs. Fletcher comes home. Did she say how long she would be staying in Oregon?"

"Mrs. Fletcher? Oh, she was kind of vaguish. The daughter's going to have a baby, and it was something about the doctor telling her she had to stay off her feet."

"Oh," Beany said; that was rather jolting news. "How much did you charge your boarder?"

Johnny shifted his burden and glanced behind him before he explained swiftly, "Beany, this guy—Ralph

31

Tyson is his name, but everyone calls him Ty—is having a pretty hard go of it. Remember my telling you about the fellow that came up here from a little town, the one I met up at the creamery on the Boul—he works there till ten at night? He has to take classes at summer school to get enough credits to enroll at the U this fall. He borrowed the creamery truck till tomorrow to move his stuff over. Yeh, he's having the darnedest time to get by—"

Beany's heart started a downward slide. She breathed out, "Oh, Johnny, I'll bet you didn't charge him enough so I can make any profit."

"Profit? Why would we want to make any profit on a fellow like that? He's going to sleep in my room. He's kind of a mixed-up fellow—star athlete and all that. And he doesn't know the first thing about settling down to the grind of studying, so I figured I could help him. Here he was, paying out room rent and buying meals on the fly and being so short of dough he only bought hamburgers now and then to fill in with the ice cream he got at the creamery."

"How much did you tell him for board?"

"I told him just what you said it cost to feed a human, that's what I told him," Johnny said shortly.

"Oh no!" Beany cried. "Not after I took in Lisa for just what the groceries will cost. Not when I had it all planned to keep boarders to make money."

"You had it all planned! Well, for John's sake, why don't you tell someone?"

"I tried to tell you," Beany said, almost in tears. "But you wouldn't listen. Nobody would listen."

Johnny gave her an odd look, just as another footstep sounded on the porch.

I won't put up with it, Beany vowed to herself. I'll just tell this poor mixed-up star athlete that the Beany Malone boarding house is not for him. He can go right on living on hamburgers and ice cream. Nobody ever starved to death on that.

Johnny opened the door for the new boarder. Beany, still holding the wall light, kept twisting the cord round and round the lamp base, while she mentally rehearsed her speech. Out of the side of her eye, she could see that, like Johnny, he had his arms full. He wore a baseball cap plus a hat on his head. An accordion was hung around his neck; he carried a canvas laundry bag, two silver trophies, a pair of shoes, and a big carton of ice cream.

"This is Beany, Ty," Johnny said.

A shoe dropped at her feet and the accordion gave out a wheezing note as the boarder shifted his load. He said, with a cocky laugh, "This wasn't my idea, to come barging in with Johnny without giving you any warning. But Johnny said you wouldn't mind, so I gathered you must be the kind of a girl everybody dreams about, but never really meets up with."

Oh, a very pretty speech, Beany thought, still twisting the lamp cord. But pretty speeches didn't pay for cherry red carpeting. I'll just tell him I'm not the kind you dream about, and that business is business—

And then she looked up and met his eyes. They were smiling at her; they were blue with dancing gold flecks in them. Her first flustered thought was: I can't believe it. I've heard of Norse gods, but I never expected one to walk in our front door.

His hair wasn't golden blond, but more of a dusty blond, as though the sun had wrung the color from it.

33

She had to tilt her head to look up at him. He was even taller than Johnny, but he hadn't Johnny's lank look. But of course, the star athlete, bringing his silver trophies along with his shirts and shoes.

Now was the time to say, and say it firmly, "I'm sorry, but I can't take any boarders unless I make a profit." Instead, she heard her voice saying, "Oh, no, I don't mind your barging in at all."

And Beany's second flustered thought was: Oh, why did I have to be wearing this faded old candy-striped blouse of Mary Fred's? And these messy pedal pushers with coffee stains on them? Why couldn't I have had on lipstick?

Ty said, "Here's some ice cream for you. At the creamery when we clean out the big containers to put in fresh ice cream, the hired help gets the old stuff. You can count on my bringing home the bacon every night— only it'll be pistachio or chocolate chip."

"Take it, Beany, and dish it up while we put all this stuff away," Johnny said. "I hope you can dig up a chunk of cake to go with it."

"Cake," said Ty with a gay whoop, and again his gold-flecked eyes smiled at Beany. "All this and heaven, too."

Beany felt her spirits lifting to his high exuberance. "Just cupcakes." She laughed and quoted, "If I'd knowed you was coming, I'da iced the cupcakes."

Late as it was, the serving of the ice cream and the un-iced cupcakes took on a party air.

Johnny said, "What's this about a new boarder? A *she?* Wake her up, Beany, and have her join us. A new girl is always a treat. What's her name?"

"Lisa," she answered. "She isn't a regular girl—I mean,

34

not the kind you'd think. She's kind of scared and bashful, and she's—well, she's fat."

"Fat or thin, she's still my baby," sang out the wise-cracking Ty.

Beany went upstairs and wakened her. "Lisa, don't you want to come down and eat ice cream with us? Johnny brought home a boy named Ty, and they told me to come up and get you."

Lisa was sitting up in bed. She seemed to shrink back. "Oh, no—no, Beany. Because I— No, I'd better not."

"But they told me to come and get you."

Johnny reinforced Beany's invitation by yelling from the foot of the stairs, "Come on, Lisa. We've got a dish of ice cream piled high for you."

And Ty added, "Slip on a smile and a robe and join the party."

The robe Lisa slipped on was one of dark maroon silk with a paisley pattern. (Off the same bolt as her grand-mother's, Beany thought again.) The smile she slipped on was a very quavery one as she followed Beany into the kitchen and was introduced to Johnny and Ty and hur-riedly shrank into a corner chair with her eyes down, as though she didn't want to see a startled look in anyone's eyes because of her size.

Yes, it was like a party. Lisa didn't add to the gaiety— or did she? Did she add just by her shy pleasure at being there? Just by her smile of appreciation at everything anyone said? She took a second helping of ice cream and cupcakes.

"Now that I know our capacity," Ty said, "I'll pack the carton tighter and higher tomorrow night."

"I'm going to make cookies tomorrow for Beany to

35

send away," Lisa said. "And I can double the recipe and have some for our ice cream."

"A cookie-maker is just what we need in our lean-to," Johnny said, flashing his warming smile at her, "so stick around for a year or two, won't you?"

Beany had known that Johnny would go out of his way to put Lisa at ease, to make her feel one of them. Johnny was instinctively chivalrous. And Ty was—well, all right. After that first shocked look at her bulges under her shapeless robe, Beany could tell that Lisa was merely a listener in the background for him.

Ty told them about himself. He had come from the town of Tyson on the Western Slope. The town had been founded by and named after his great-grandfather. "Hick town, if you ever saw one. I took it until I couldn't take any more of it, and then I packed my grip and blew. That was last April—April Fool's day, in fact, and s'help us, I'll never put foot in that burg again."

"Do your folks live there?" Beany asked; she still felt a little fluttery at the thought of this boy with the cocky laugh and the gold-flecked eyes being under their own roof.

"My dad was killed in the war. Mom's still there. She's in the school library. And, of course, the Tysons have shirt-tail relatives all over the place."

Johnny said, "Must give you a kind of big-shot feeling to be a Tyson that the town was named after."

Ty got up from the table and lit a cigarette as though some restlessness kept him from sitting quietly. "A lot that means to people out there now! That's what I said to Mom—that when it got to the point where Tysons were pushed around in their own town—" He tossed his head. "Me, I don't push easy."

36

5

THE next day Lisa, with Beany showing her where the ingredients were, made cookies to send to Andy Kern. A double recipe of panocha fudge cookies with black walnuts. Cut into squares, they packed nicely into a shoe box. Beany said as she wrapped it, "I'll mail it downtown tomorrow."

When she took the bus downtown the following morning, she wore her snug-fitting and slightly scratchy swim suit under her blouse and skirt. For Ty, with no classes on Saturday morning, had said, "How about all of us going over to the park for a swim? How about your joining us after you mail your package, Beany, and making like a mermaid?"

It just might be that she wouldn't be wearing this old swim suit home.

For there had been a full-page ad in the morning *Call* devoted to "Seaside Drama." Beany's eyes had rested covetously on them. "The new, romantic, glamorous, swimsilhouette." She couldn't very well make like a mermaid in a two-year-old suit that had been a basement bargain to begin with. Ty was just a boarder—but, after all, a landlady didn't have to be a "drab," did she?

She went to the post office in the basement of the department store to mail the cookies. And there she felt a sudden matchmaking itch. She stopped at one of the long counters and, taking a stubby pen, added Lisa's name in the corner so that it read, "From Beany Malone and Lisa Hold." She added to the address so that it read, "To: Pfc. Andy Kern and Pfc. Joe Kaswell."

Be nice if the bashful "Kansas" would send a message to Lisa through Andy.

She was still undecided about the new swim suit. No, that was too much money to spend for vanity. Nosir, she had dedicated her summer to a new rumpus room. The old suit would have to do. . . . Still, it wouldn't hurt to *look* at them.

She stopped at the counter displaying Seaside Drama, and one look convinced her that her old one under her blouse and skirt was not fit to be seen in. She bought a turquoise blue. She went to the ladies' room, swiftly peeled off the dreary one she was wearing, and put on her clothes over the new one.

When she reached the sandy beach at the park she found Lisa and Johnny waiting impatiently and hungrily for her. Johnny had just come out of the water, and was shaking his dark head like a spaniel. Lisa wore her usual dark skirt and one of those unflattering, grandmothery blouses—buttons down the front, sleeves that were neither short nor long, too much fullness gathered onto the yoke. If only she could get into one of Beany's or Mary Fred's!

Johnny said, "I wanted to rent Lisa a suit so she could go in."

38

Lisa squirmed sheepishly. "I thought I'd better watch the towels and shoes and lunch. I don't like to swim."

As though Beany didn't know she meant, I don't like to be seen in a swim suit. And Beany didn't wonder.

Johnny hallooed to Ty who was over at the diving board. Eeks! Beany had been right. A Norse god in his blue boxer shorts. She hurried out of her blouse and skirt, pretending she was stifling with the heat and not at all anxious to show off what was underneath.

Ty's dusty blond hair didn't plaster down like most boys' when it was wet. He was running his fingers through it as he picked his way among the groups on the beach. Beany noticed the eyes that were turned his way.

It was worth having paid the price of three yards of red carpeting for her suit when he gave a low whistle and said, "Lorelei! What wave washed you to shore?"

Even sandwiches, tomatoes, and potato chips tasted better when a girl wore a "glamorous swimsilhouette." Ty mentioned, almost too casually, "I won the high-diving championship in a meet one year. We had a natural lake near Tyson."

A perfect afternoon. A breeze robbed the June sun of its heat. Johnny stretched out on a dampish towel and pulled a book and notebook toward him. He asked Ty, "Did you bring your books? How about some help on your Monday assignments?"

Ty laughed. "Monday's a long way off—and the water's just right. Besides, I promised a fellow to coach him on his half-gainer." He stood up. "I'm going back in."

Beany got up, too, and they went in the water together. She had trouble keeping up with him as he swam with masterful ease out to the rope that marked off the deep area. She clung to it, quite out of breath. Swimming, to

Beany's crowd, meant fifteen minutes in the water to an hour on the beach.

Ty swam far out in the lake while Beany held on to the swaying rope. He circled back to her and asked, "How about going over and trying some dives?"

Beany was no diver. But, after all, you couldn't blame a champion for wanting to be with the more fearless who took their turns off the tower.

"You go ahead. I'm going in and sun and visit with Lisa. And I see one of my friends from Harkness High."

The friend was Dulcie Lungaarde. She was a pert and pretty girl who worked as carhop at the Ragged Robin drive-in on the Boulevard. She was sitting on a purple-striped beach robe that matched her suit, smearing suntan lotion on her arms and legs. She took off a fancy pair of sunglasses and squinted up at Beany.

"Hm'm, I see you invested in Seaside Drama, too. I chose this purple patch because I thought it would draw all eyes in my direction. I'm not going in the water. I won't have time to get my crowning beauty wet and then dry again, before I start juggling trays at the Robin."

Her crowning beauty was indeed that. It was the color of burnt sugar and she wore it in a pony tail that cascaded out and down like a plume. She also wore eye make-up, which emphasized the blue of her eyes and her petal skin.

Beany said, "Come on over to our blanket. Johnny's there, reading up on some old-timer, no doubt. I want you to meet Lisa, who's staying with us for a while."

"You mean that overfed number with Johnny? I wondered what the score was. I wondered if he was so hard put for a girl since Miggs Carmody left town that he— Where in the world did she come from? And why doesn't she reduce? She doesn't have to be *that* much of an eyeful."

40

"Hush, Dulcie, she might hear you. She's from Wichita —and she's sensitive about being so fat. She says it runs in the family and she can't do a thing about it."

"Except eat, I suppose."

Johnny lifted his dark absorbed eyes from his book, said, "Hi, Dulcie. Hey, I've just got a swell idea for our old-time TV program. We're going to use the night the train finally chugged into Denver City in 1870—"

"Oh-oh, the snows of yesteryear," Beany murmured. "Who'd you come with, Dulcie?"

"A muscle-bound All-American who stopped by our house. Him, in the plaid trunks, showing off on the high diving board."

Lisa said unexpectedly, "Beany's boarder is doing the same."

"Beany, are you really taking in boarders?" Dulcie asked. "I thought you were just talking to hear your head rattle that day I called and you said you were going to work your fingers to the bone so as to Jennifer-Reed up a room in the basement."

Beany said stiffly, "I'm going to take three more boarders. I'm going to buy the paint this afternoon and start fixing up a rumpus room." Dulcie didn't need to call it Jennifer-Reeding.

"This is my idea," Johnny put in. "Do you realize that practically all our pioneers who trekked across the plains either were seeking something or running away from something?"

"Which one is your boarder, Beany?" Dulcie asked.

"In the bright blue trunks. There, he's just doing a jackknife."

"Um-mm-mm," Dulcie said, smacking her reddened lips meaningfully. "Mr. Wonderful. Him I must look over."

Johnny said, "We have ice-cream socials every night at the Malones', shortly after ten when Ty arrives with the wherewithal. You are cordially invited to join us when you get off work tonight."

"I'll come a-runnin'," Dulcie promised, "and bring Norbett, the almost Old Faithful."

Beany's heart gave only a small wince at that. Norbett, who was now Dulcie's almost Old Faithful, had been Beany's first beau. Yet she had to admit that Dulcie could handle the moody, unpredictable, redheaded Norbett Rhodes better than she ever could. "Norbett's sulks and tantrums don't bother me," Dulcie always said.

Johnny was saying, "Yeh, we'll have all the whoop-te-do of that first night when the train pulled into Denver. But you see, it will be a different slant if we focus on the runners-away and their dreading to see the train come, because they didn't want any connection with the past and whatever they were running away from—"

Dulcie said, "Hey, Beany, when is Jennifer Reed going to have her farewell-Jennifer, welcome-Beany party? I can hardly wait, seein' as how it will be my first attendance as a staff member." She turned to Johnny and Lisa with a knowing smile. "Maybe Beany doesn't know that I know that she's responsible for my being on the *Hark Ye* staff. Can't you just imagine loyal old Beany cramming me down the throats of the other worthy members?"

Beany flushed and said, "Oh, Dulcie!" But Dulcie's flippant remark was uncomfortably near the truth. She had never been accepted at Harkness High because of her very brashness. Beany *had* been instrumental in getting Dulcie a toehold on the staff as one of the reporters at large.

Beany murmured, "Jennifer Reed wanted you, too, Dulcie."

"She's a good gal," Dulcie said soberly. "Wait till you see the new house the Reeds are moving to. It's that delectable pink-painted brick in Harmony Heights. Dad's been doing some carpenter work for Papa Reed out there—new doors on the garage or some such."

"Won't anybody listen to me?" Johnny yelled.

"I'll listen, Johnny," Lisa said. "I want to hear about the train and the runners-away."

"There's a gal," he bragged. "Lisa, you remind me of something I read once. It was a poem and I can't remember just how it went, but the idea was that there are two ways of spreading light. One, like the candle that glows. And one like the mirror that reflects the light. Lisa, you listen, you reflect, you bolster souls."

Lisa's eyes lighted in gratitude. Dulcie snorted, "I don't want to be anybody's mirror. I want to do my own shining." And Beany said, "You're a fine one, Johnny, to talk about listening and bolstering souls. Just day before yesterday when I needed a bolsterer, all you could think of was some old character named Soapy Smith."

Dulcie said, "Beany, you've got forty-two more freckles across your nose. Daub on some of this suntan lotion."

Time passed quickly. Dulcie and her high diver left. The afternoon was well along when Ty, panting and spent, rejoined them.

It was too late by the time they reached home for Beany and Lisa to fix supper for him. He had to be at his creamery job by five thirty. "Don't you worry," he said to Beany with his bright smile. "I'll catch up on a hamburger or two when I get home."

Johnny said, "Let's just eat enough to hold us now, and then have hamburgers cooked on the fireplace in the backyard when Ty arrives."

6

BEANY drove to the boulevard for the Saturday special on hamburger. And then she stopped at the hardware store to buy paint for the walls of the wine room. She fell into the hands of an earnest-eyed clerk who took her paint problems onto his own rounded shoulders. He had once been a painter himself, he told her, and any room was just as successful as its paint job.

So that when Beany said vaguely that she wanted about a gallon of oyster white and maybe a gallon of forest green, he asked her the dimensions of the walls and ceiling to be painted. She could only tell him the dimensions of the floor she had walked off a few nights ago. Using those figures, he did a great deal of arithmetic, pausing only to ask her what *kind* of walls she was buying paint for.

"They're brick. No, not glazed—just old and rough brick."

That brought about a thoughtful pursing of lips. Then she should buy masonry paint—at least five gallons. And she would need special brushes for the rough brick walls. She would need paint cleaner for the brushes—"and for the painters," he added with a chuckle.

Somehow, Beany had thought of the paint as a small incidental in the transforming of the wine room into a rumpus room. She had no idea that it would take so much, or that paint cost so much. Or that brushes, especially the durable, stiff-bristled kind for use on rough walls, were so expensive. The adding machine in the hardware store totaled almost thirty dollars.

She didn't have enough money. She had snatched up only a twenty-dollar bill out of the oatmeal box before leaving.

The clerk asked, "You're one of the Malones, aren't you?"

"Yes, I'm Beany Malone."

"Then it's perfectly all right for you to pay me the rest later on. I'll load your paint in your car, so you'll have it to start work with. You stop by any time and finish paying for it."

"I'll be in Monday," she said.

What a dent this purchase would make in her Sinking Fund. But then it wouldn't be long before she'd have more board money to deposit in the oatmeal box.

Someone called to her as she started out of the store. It was a woman in a housedress, with her nose red and peeling from outdoor work in the yard. It was Mrs. Kern, mother of Andy Kern whose joining the Marines had left such a gap in Beany's life. Mrs. Kern was looking at garden tools, and Beany stopped to visit with her. They compared the latest news from Andy.

"How is Rosellen?" Beany asked.

Rosellen was Andy's sixteen-year-old sister. She had

45

gone through a serious bout with polio as a child and had progressed gradually from her bed to a wheelchair, from the wheelchair to crutches.

"She's out in the car," Mrs. Kern said; something dark and worrying flitted across her sunburned face. "She misses Andy so. You know what a fuss he always made over her."

Yes, Beany knew. She thought of the times on their dates when Andy would say, "Got to get to Downey's Drug before it closes for ice cream for Rosellen." Other times Rosellen would be with them. If there were steps, Andy would hand Beany the crutches, gather Rosellen up in his arms and carry her up or down, pretending all the while that he was about to drop her. And when Beany would say, "Here are your crutches, Rosellen," Andy would gasp out, "I'm the one that needs crutches."

Mrs. Kern added, "Beany, I'm afraid her bad leg is bothering her. Of course, she doesn't complain. She can't bear for anyone to feel sorry for her."

"I know," Beany murmured.

"She's out in the car, honey. Stop and say hello to her."

On the sidewalk, Beany's eyes sorted through the cars at the curb until she recognized the Kern family car in which she had ridden so often with Andy. It was parked in front of a small dress shop. There was Rosellen in the front seat. How pretty she was, with her dark mane of curly hair, her eyes that crinkled when she smiled.

But she wasn't smiling now. It was the first time Beany had ever seen her sitting quietly and alone and, as she thought, unobserved. Her eyes were on the display of sport clothes in the shop window. One manikin in shorts and bright yellow T shirt held an uplifted tennis racket. Another, in a sleeveless checked dress, had its two stiff hands

46

clasped around a golf club. Still another, in frilly swim suit, lolled in a deck chair.

Beany looked back at Rosellen's wistful face. . . . Johnny Malone had said once, "Sometimes you have a feeling of angels clutching at Rosellen's sleeve." . . . Beany knew such an ache of sympathy that she moved swiftly toward her.

Her one idea was to expel the sadness in the girl's face. "Hi there, Rosellen. Say, how'd you like to come to an outdoor supper at our house tonight?"

Rosellen looked at her. It was as though a lamp went on, lighting up her eyes. Her laugh was a trill of joy.

"A party at the Malones'! Oh, wonderful."

"It'll be kind of late because this boy who's staying with us doesn't get off work until ten."

Again Rosellen laughed spontaneously. "It's never too late to go to a party. Just as soon as Mom buys her hoe and we go home, I'll call Sidney—you want Sidney too, don't you?—and tell him to come over and get me. In case he's on the elevator at the Park Gate tonight, he can trade hours with someone else."

Sidney Peale was Rosellen's Old Faithful—and no *almost* about it. He was an English boy in Beany's class at Harkness High, who was sure to be the class valedictorian when they graduated next year. For Sidney was a "brain" and the delight of every teacher. He and his parents lived in the basement apartment at the Park Gate, a luxury hotel and apartment house. Sidney's father was the caretaker, and Sidney himself was one of the elevator pilots.

Rosellen Kern and Sidney Peale made a perfect pair. When Beany first knew Sidney he had been painfully shy and reserved and lacking in self-confidence. If ever, Beany often thought, that "you're so wonderful" technique ac-

47

complished miracles it was on Sidney Peale. It worked both ways, too. For the adoration in Sidney's eyes gave Rosellen a feeling that one of the opposite sex found her desirable, even though she must always occupy an aisle seat at movies and sit out dances.

But only Rosellen's body sat on the sidelines of life. Like her brother Andy, she loved people, music, fun. Her spirit danced along, unhampered by crutches.

She said now, "I wish I'd known about your party sooner so I could have brought a cake. I've got a new recipe."

"Maybe next time," Beany said. It was good to see Rosellen her old bubbling-over self.

"Beany, what about Jennifer Reed's party? She ought to be all moved and settled pretty soon, oughtn't she? When she has it, can the staff bring their dates?"

Rosellen was not, of course, on the *Hark Ye* staff; she was not even a student at Harkness. She went to a small private school where stairs were no problem. But Sidney Peale was one of the *Hark Ye*'s new staff members.

"I don't know about the dates," Beany said, feeling a tinge of discomfort. Somehow, you didn't think of a party at the Reed house in Harmony Heights as one of those "the more, the merrier" kind, rumpus room or no.

"Golly, I hope she'll tell the staff to bring dates," Rosellen sighed. She went on, "Sidney was just treading on air when he told me he was to be on the *Hark Ye* staff as some sort of adviser to the finance editor." Again Rosellen's laugh of delight. "Poor old Sidney is so smart he's dumb. I didn't tell him that I saw the fine hand of Beany Malone in his getting there."

The eyes of the two girls met in understanding. Tears welled into Rosellen's eyes; she was the only one Beany knew who could laugh one minute and cry the next. "Oh,

48

Beany, you're wonderful and I love you. That sweet old stand-offish Sidney! I could just imagine you setting your square jaw and saying to the staff, 'We've been overlooking someone we ought to have, and that's Sidney Peale.'"

Beany laughed. That was almost exactly what she had said. For, just as it had hurt her to see Dulcie left out of school activities because of her boldness, so had she hated to see Sidney left out because of his shyness.

Mrs. Kern came up then with her sharp-pointed hoe; and, as Beany parted from them, Rosellen said happily, "See you tonight."

The Saturday-night supper at the Malones' got off to a late but happy and noisy start. Ty came hurrying home and dumped down his carton of ice cream with a rumbling growl. "I'm hungry as a werewolf, whatever a werewolf is," he announced.

Dulcie and Norbett arrived. She changed out of her carhop togs—the white boots, short red skirt, and gold-trimmed jacket—into a flowered sunback dress in Beany's room. She was in high spirits. She struck a pose and gestured toward the cloudy sky. "Moon! Moon! Keep shining in June."

Beany, helping Johnny with the hamburgers on the outdoor fireplace, watched to see if Ty and Dulcie would gravitate toward each other. She wondered how the red-headed, moody Norbett would take it if Ty did. However he took it, whether with sulks or temper, Dulcie would pay little heed.

But Ty didn't seem bowled over by Dulcie's pert charm.

Lisa was just handing around the hamburgers in buns when the thud of Rosellen's crutches announced her and Sidney's arrival. Every boy in the Malone backyard hurried to find the most comfortable chair for her, to open a bottle of coke for her. Johnny asked, "Do you like your hamburger well burned or slightly scorched?" Norbett said, "How about ice in your coke? I can scoot in the kitchen and get some."

Queer, Beany thought, how Rosellen brought out the chivalry in every male. More than that, she had some magic of pulling a group together, of giving everyone a feeling of loving-kindness toward each other. Even the edgy Norbett was more relaxed and his edges rounded when she was in the group.

This evening he kept pushing up to Beany, offering, "Here, I'll do that for you." Queer, too, what a stormy session she and Norbett Rhodes had gone through when they had been near-steadies at Harkness High. But now he played the role of an ex-boy-friend who is just a loyal well-wisher. He even asked, "What do you hear from Andy Kern these days?"

Imagine that! After Norbett's jealous tantrums when she had first started dating Andy. In those days Norbett hadn't even referred to him as Andy Kern but as "the policeman's son," because his father was Captain Kern of the Auto Theft Department.

Beany answered, "He's had his leave after boot training, so I don't suppose he'll be getting back for a while."

It grew harder to find the salt and the dill pickles as the clouds slid over the moon and the night grew darker. Beany brought out a candelabrum from the living-room mantel, but a gust of wind snuffed out all three candles. She and Lisa had to feel for the dishes when they served the ice cream; and Ty, misjudging the edge of the outdoor table, spilled his in his lap.

"We ought to have hurricane lights," Beany said.

"I'll tell you what we ought to have," Ty answered. "One of those flares in a black pot they use to mark roadblocks. They burn crude oil and it'd take a cyclone to blow one out."

"I remember seeing a whole row of them on a detour when I took Father Hugh up to Twin Pine," Beany murmured.

Ty brought out his accordion. They all sang lustily to his playing of old hillbilly songs and new Hit Parade tunes. They teased Johnny about his singing, out-of-tune and off-key. It didn't bother Johnny. It surprised Beany to hear Sidney's strong and true tenor (with a very British accent) rise above the others. And through it all, Lisa, a dark lump of a girl, sat with a contented smile on her face as though she were happy to be a part of it.

Under cover of the music, Dulcie Lungaarde leaned over to say to Beany, "Lucky you!" She nodded toward Ty. "Mr. Yum-yum. He wouldn't be bad to go dancing with. And to think he just dropped into your lap."

"Oh, Dulcie! Just because he's staying with us—"

"You don't want to mope around at home because Andy Kern joined the Marines, do you? You fall to and set the fair-haired boy's heart to fluttering," she advised, and joined the singing.

The next day, Sunday, was also like a house party. Johnny's waffle breakfast after Mass; a swim in the park lake. Another backyard supper. This was not so late in starting, for on Sunday night Ty got off earlier at the creamery and Dulcie left the Ragged Robin at eight. Dulcie brought barbecued spareribs from the drive-in, and Rosellen brought a cake.

And Sidney Peale brought the music of an old English

51

folk song for Ty to play on the accordion. But Ty would no sooner fasten his eyes on the music and start to play than the candles would be blown out.

Once, as Beany tried to relight them, he said, "Beany, let's you and I go out some dark night and bring us home a highway flare."

Beany didn't know what to answer. She didn't want to sound prissy and say, That's one thing Dad has dinged into us—that helping yourself to something like that is stealing. She stammered, "Well—I—I—"

But it was as though he read her thoughts, for he said mockingly, "I suppose your father lays down the laws as to what a nice little girl should or shouldn't do, and so you wouldn't dare."

"I didn't say that," Beany defended. "It's just that—"

"Skip it," he said shortly. "Just once I'd like to find a girl that wasn't the father-ridden kind, so that she could do something on her own."

Before Beany could answer, Sidney led off on the lengthy and rollicking song about old MacDonald who had a farm with every conceivable and noisy brand of livestock on it.

They all joined in, each trying to outdo the other. . . . The idea of Ty accusing her of being father-ridden. . . . It wasn't until the *baa-baas,* the *oink-oinks,* and the *quack-quacks* became louder and more realistic that she roused from her abstraction. "Turn the volume down," she cautioned. "We've got neighbors, you know."

"Just two," Dulcie said. "And they could stand a little music in their souls."

The hilarious song went on.

To the south of the Malones lived Mrs. Adams. The

52

young folks called her Mrs. Socially-Prominent Adams, because her teas and her serving on hospital and symphony boards always rated her picture or a write-up on the society page.

The massive dark brick to the north was the home of the Buell family. Carlton, the Buells' only child, was Johnny's best friend. If he were home, he would be here with them. But Carlton was counseling at a boys' camp in the mountains this summer.

Beany had often thought of how houses took on the personality of their owners. Mrs. Adams's colonial house, with its white ruffled curtains at every window and its window boxes of petunias, had the same coy prettiness, the same well-groomed look as its owner.

The Buell house had somehow taken on the stern and judicial look of the judge himself. It had no front porch; its front door was heavy and forbidding. Its hedge was high enough for privacy and was always squarely trimmed. Of course, the hedge that separated Malone and Buell grounds had an opening where Johnny and Carlton went back and forth. And the Buell backyard was full of flowers, which Mrs. Buell delighted in tending and in giving away.

And in between sat the Malone house with its wide porches, its big yard, its scuffed door that was never locked. It had neither a well-groomed look nor a stern, judicial one, but an inviting "come as you are" air about it.

As the singing went on, Beany glanced uneasily at the dark silhouette of the Buell house. There was something so forbidding about Judge Buell. She wasn't at all sure that his soul needed music at this late hour.

7

ON Monday afternoon, Beany pushed her wire cart ahead of her at the supermarket on the boulevard. As yet she was not a landlady with a full table of boarders. Johnny had reported that summer-school students would not be registering until a week from today.

She reached for lemons; it took so many for iced tea. Her eyes rested on the lush redness of strawberries. No, no. Rhubarb was cheaper.

She moved on, but her eyes turned longingly back to the strawberries. It would be nice to have them as topping for the ice cream Ty brought home every evening. She knew it was extravagant, but she reached for two boxes of the berries and put them in her wire cart.

Funny, how that "ice-cream social" in the late evening gave a lift to the day. They all built their days around it. Ty had to be at the creamery at five-thirty. It made such an early dinner that he said, "Just give me enough to last until I get home, and then I'll stoke up."

Then they all stoked up, which actually made a fourth meal at the Malones'.

Something cheap and filling, Beany reminded herself again as she came to the long meat counter. This time her eyes lit on the fryers. Lamb stew would be cheaper, but you could hardly serve lamb stew for a late-at-night snack in the yard. And fryers *were* on special today. She put two in her basket.

She consulted her list. Marshmallows for toasting. Chocolate chips for cookies. H'mm, they'd gone up since last time. Cokes. And no use taking home a few. She piled in four cartons.

At the check stand the white ribbon of paper that came out of the adding machine totaled an amount that was more than Beany expected. But next week, when she was feeding real boarders—yes, next week would be time enough for her to be a dollar-minded landlady in earnest.

When she drove home with the groceries, she stopped in the driveway behind Father Hugh's hard-used car. There was Father Hugh, sitting at the outdoor table in the shade of the buckeye tree with Johnny. They both came to help her carry in her weighty sacks and cartons, while Lisa held the porch door open.

In the kitchen, Beany and Lisa stacked supplies in cupboards and refrigerator. Johnny opened cokes and passed them around, and resumed his talk with Father Hugh. Beany might have known—Johnny was still bringing the first train into Denver City.

"So don't you think, Padre, it would be sort of poignant, even tragic, if we focused on these runners-away, watching with desperate eyes every piece of rail that was laid? For the rails would make their pasts catch up with them—"

"Train or no train," Father Hugh said gruffly, "they couldn't run away from themselves. Beany, make me a cup of coffee. I don't like this sweet slop." He shoved the coke bottle across the table.

Beany put on coffee for him. Johnny left to set the sprinkler on Mrs. Fletcher's lawn before he went on to the campus library.

Lisa was folding the sacks when Father Hugh turned his deep-set, knowing eyes on her and asked, "And what are you running away from, child? Johnny tells me you came out here from Wichita to visit a relative who wasn't home."

Lisa darted a frightened look at him, and then at Beany. Feeling a surge of protectiveness for her, Beany answered, "She isn't exactly running away—that is, her folks knew she was coming out to see her father's Cousin Josie. She's just staying here until Mrs. Fletcher comes back."

"I won't go home," Lisa said. "I like it here. My folks don't want me around—they're so glad I'm gone."

"Now, now," he reproved. "In these family rows there's usually something to be said on each side. Are you sure now you're putting the blame where it belongs? It's always easier to blame the other fellow."

"Her sister didn't want her for a bridesmaid," Beany retorted. "I'd run away, too, if my sister said I'd turn the whole wedding into a farce, and that I'd be a laughing-stock because I was so fat."

"Did she actually tell you that?" the priest asked Lisa.

"Not to me," Lisa said chokily, "but I heard her saying it to Mother."

Beany saw the flash of sympathy in Father Hugh's eyes, heard his muttered, "Humph!" He waited until she put the coffee before him and then lifted one interrogative eyebrow. "Tell me this, Lisa, do your folks know that you're here at the Malones', instead of with this aunt or cousin, whatever her name is?"

"Mrs. Fletcher," Beany supplied.

"No, they don't know but what I'm at Cousin Josie's," Lisa admitted.

"That's bad," he scolded. "Supposing they tried to phone you? Supposing they heard from this relative in Oregon? They'd be frantic with worry." He got to his feet and said, as though Lisa were eight instead of nearly eighteen, "You get right in there to the telephone and call them up. We'll have no more of this dodging around. Come on now."

Lisa could only give Beany a hopeless and helpless look as Father Hugh ushered her into the hall. "I don't want to talk to them," Lisa kept repeating. "They'll just tell me to come back—and I won't."

"Then I'll talk to them," Father Hugh said. "Dial O, and give Long Distance your Wichita number."

But, as it happened, Lisa didn't have to talk to her folks, and Father Hugh didn't have a chance to. There was no answer. Lisa looked up from the telephone to say, "The operator wants to know if she should try again in twenty minutes."

He said thoughtfully, "Tell her no. I'm leaving as soon as I drink my coffee. Let me have the number and I'll phone them from Twin Pine."

"Will you be sure and tell them that I like it here, and I don't want to go home?" Lisa insisted.

The priest gave her a rueful smile. "I never know what I'm going to tell anyone till I get started," he said.

A caller came to the Malone house that evening. It was Judge Buell, their neighbor to the north.

His son Carlton would never think of coming to the front door and ringing the bell. He always took the beaten path to their back door. Nor did the busy and friendly Mrs. Buell, who visited with them across the hedge, come to the front door when she brought bouquets of her flowers to them.

But Judge Buell was not the type to cut across lawns or visit over a hedge. He always wore dark suits and white shirts and somber ties. It even surprised Beany that the judge and her father were such good friends, and that her father called him "Joe" as though he were an ordinary human. Beany had said once to Johnny, "Judge Buell seems *older* than most fathers."

"He is," Johnny had answered. "That's because he didn't marry until he was what he terms 'established.' He's always sounding off about the responsibilities of marriage to Carlton and me. Maybe that's why poor old Carl is so girl-shy he ends up by asking Beany Malone to the hops at the U." Johnny had grinned. "He feels as safe with you as with his maiden aunt."

Beany had widened her eyes in mock innocence. "You mean you didn't know that Carlton keeps begging me to elope with him?"

This evening Beany answered the door with a tea towel in her hand. She answered the judge's formal, "Good evening, Beany," with a flustered, "Oh, hello—good evening, Judge," and thought: What in the world is he coming over for?

But she remembered her manners and asked him in. He sat down stiffly and waited until Beany disposed not only of her tea towel, but a pair of soggy beach shoes Johnny had left on the couch, and sat down opposite him. Then he cleared his throat.

Beany's mind flashed back to the time when, in junior high, her Current Events class had visited a courtroom. Judge Buell in his black robes was presiding. She remembered his stern rapping on the desk, his, "Order in the courtroom!"

He said now, "I have a little matter to talk over with you and Johnny."

"Johnny isn't here. I think he's timing Friday's TV script with the professor."

Could the little matter be a complaint about their noisy and hilarious evening in the Malone yard? Beany said uneasily, "I hope we haven't kept you awake with the accordion and our singing."

He put up his hand for silence as though she were talking out of turn. He cleared his throat again and said, "Your father spoke to me the evening before he left and asked me if, in case of any emergency, I would take care of it during his absence."

Beany knew relief. "That's nice of you, Judge Buell. But we're getting along fine. We—that is, I decided to keep a few boarders this summer."

"Young people, I gather. I noticed a young woman about the premises. Is she one of them?"

Beany felt her defenses stiffen. "Her name is Lisa Hold, and she's from Wichita." She had a feeling that the less Judge Buell knew about Lisa's sudden decision to come to Denver, the better.

"And this young man I see coming in and out? Am I to gather that he is a boarder also?"

Beany nodded. "His name is Ralph Tyson. He's from a little town named Tyson that was named for his grandfather or maybe his great-grandfather. He's going to summer school so he can enter the U this fall, and he works nights at a creamery. He's very nice."

The judge harumphed a few times before he queried further, "Are you—er—keeping company with him?"

"Oh, no. No, I never saw him before Johnny brought him home."

What an old-fashioned expression, "keeping company." Yet that was what Dulcie had advised her to do, as long as Andy Kern was far away, and Ty had dropped into her lap—

Judge Buell interrupted her thoughts with a more vigorous than usual clearing of his throat; Beany caught herself doing the same. He said, "Beany, I'm cognizant of the fact that you—yes, and Johnny—have been merely thoughtless, let us say, in taking in these young people. But a house of unchaperoned teen-agers is a bit unconventional even in these days."

Beany started to speak, but again he gave her a silencing look as though she were the culprit at the bar.

"I'd feel that I was failing in my promise to your father to let this matter go on. It could occasion talk in the neighborhood. The appearance of wrongdoing can be just as disastrous as—as—" He paused, groping for the right word.

"But they're here—Lisa and Ty. We can't get rid of them," she expostulated. And she thought, I'm seventeen, and *practically* an adult. Why can't old fogies let us run our own lives?

"That wouldn't be necessary if you had an adult in the house. My suggestion is that you get in an older house-keeper and have her live here in the house with you."

Beany said aghast, "We couldn't do that, Judge Buell. She'd take up an extra room—and, goodness, you know what housekeepers cost. It would take all my profit. I mean, my whole idea was to keep boarders to make money so I could turn the wine room in the basement into a rumpus room."

"Did you discuss these plans of yours with your parents?"

"Well—no, I didn't have a chance to, because I just decided the night before they left. But I wrote to Adair and Dad and told them about Lisa staying here until—" no, she wouldn't mention Mrs. Fletcher because that would only bring on more catechizing. "Yes, I wrote them that I was going to keep boarders and fix up the rumpus room. You know how Dad is. He's always believed in letting us go ahead when we wanted to do something to get something we wanted."

"I'm sure your parents wouldn't approve of an unchaperoned houseful of young folks," he stated dogmatically.

They were getting nowhere, Beany realized. She realized, too, that the judge was firmly implanted on the couch and had no intention of leaving until they—or he—did get somewhere.

After a long silence, she suggested hopefully, "I could call up the Housing Office on the campus and ask them if they had a sort of middle-aged teacher they could send—or maybe an older student. Last summer I used to see some of the summer-school students at Downey's Drug, and a few of them were kind of old."

The judge seemed to be turning that over in his mind.

61

"Yes," he said at last, "that might solve the problem very nicely if you had an older person here—one with a sobering influence." Praise be, he was getting to his feet and moving toward the door. "But I think it might be better if I dropped into the Housing Office on my way downtown in the morning and talked to the person who handles the placements." A long-drawn rumbling in his throat. "Yes, I'll attend to that."

"Thank you, Judge Buell," Beany managed to say, even as she thought irritably: I'd feel sorry for the girl Carlton Buell marries. The judge would probably think he had to "attend to" everything from the picking out of the ring to buying a bathroom mat.

8

IT was typical of Johnny Malone that, even though he could not understand or appreciate Beany's longing for a private rumpus room, he would still pitch in and help her acquire it.

"Holy mud, Beany," he said the next morning when he went to the basement with her and Lisa and pried the lids off a gallon bucket of white paint and another of dark green, "why sink a lot of dough in this dreary hole?"

"Because I want a place where I can hold private staff meetings," she said.

"Listen to her, Lisa. Private staff meetings! Meaning that she doesn't want her brother Johnny butting in. I'm getting that unwanted feeling. I'll develop a warped personality and go through life biting old ladies."

"Oh, Johnny, it's just that Jennifer—well, our staff really did get a lot more work done when we didn't have a lot of interruptions."

63

"All right, all right, if it's uninterrupted hours in a basement you hanker for! I'll cart in the stepladder and do the ceiling and all the high spots. So swaddle yourselves and the floor, because some of the paint will go on the ceiling, but a lot will come down."

They wrapped their heads and dressed in the oldest clothes they could find; they covered the floor with newspapers. Johnny set up the unsteady ladder that squeaked and chirped under his weight.

The ladder even screeched when, in mid-morning, he descended it hurriedly and bounded up the stairs to answer the telephone. He returned to the paint-smelly basement room to announce, "That was Judge Buell."

Beany turned on her high stool, her green paint brush poised. "What'd he say?"

"He wished to report," said Johnny, imitating the judge, "that he has arranged for a very estimable Miss Rutledge to take up residence at Beany's Beanery."

Lisa giggled. "I'll bet he didn't say Beanery."

"Then he *did* go to the Housing Office," Beany muttered. "Then he *did* find someone to have a sobering influence on us all. I was in hopes he'd forget."

"An elephant or Judge Buell never forgets," Johnny said.

"What else did he say about—what's her name again?"

"Rutledge." Johnny went through a series of throat clearings again and quoted the judge, " 'She sounds like a most commendable person. She teaches third and fourth grades out in Farady—' That's wheat country," Johnny said in his own voice, " 'and she devotes her summers to acquiring a master's degree in literature—harumph, harumph—so that she needs a room to herself to do the reading and the writing of papers which—' "

64

"Yuck, yuck! Then we'll have to give her Dad's and Adair's room. There go my two nice young men I was going to put in there."

"Maybe they wouldn't have been so nice," Johnny said. "Maybe one would drink sauerkraut juice for breakfast, and the other would elope with Lisa here."

"Johnny!" Lisa scolded.

"Did he say how old this Rutledge woman is?" Beany put in.

"No, and I think that worries the judge because he didn't see her birth certificate. But at the Housing Office they assured him that she was well past the giddy age. So, feeling that we would be very fortunate in having Miss Rutledge, he took the liberty of phoning her that Beany Malone would put out the red carpet in welcome."

"We can't put out or down the red carpet," Beany said with a rueful laugh, "until Miss Rutledge pays for it. It still burns me that Judge Buell took it on himself to get someone. I dread to think of what she'll be like."

Lisa said, "I was crazy about my third-grade teacher. She was always having us write poems. I still remember one little boy writing,

'My mother is queer
She don't like beer.' "

The painting was hard work, but fun. Lisa laughed at everything Johnny said. They took turns at going upstairs and bringing back cokes or lemonade. They tossed a coin to see who should scrub up and fix lunch.

In between his morning classes and his evening job at the creamery, Ty even painted part of the ceiling while Johnny took Lisa to a downtown bank to cash her government bonds. She paid Beany for two weeks' board.

But Ty didn't stick to his painting long. After about half an hour, he said to Beany, "Think I'll sprint over to the park and swim a while. Got to keep in trim for when the coach at the U looks me over for football."

After all, Beany told herself, you couldn't expect a boarder, even a nonprofit one, to take on an onerous painting job.

And onerous it was. The bricks were rough; they slowed the brushes and wore down the bristles. They were porous, too; they soaked up paint like sponges. Beany began to wonder if her five gallons of paint would cover walls and ceiling.

They painted all that day. They ate sandwiches and ice cream when Ty came home in the evening, and groaned from sore muscles as they climbed the stairs to bed.

On Thursday, a letter came to Johnny from Mrs. Fletcher. She wanted him to cut back the iris when they were finished blooming, and to spray the rose bushes. She added that she couldn't say when she would be home, because Martha had to stay off her feet.

"Martha has a little boy who's about two," Lisa said.

Johnny grinned at her, "Well, Lisa, looks like you're going to be stuck with us Malones for a while."

Lisa turned troubled eyes to Beany. "I guess you'd rather I didn't stay on, so you could rent my room for more money."

"Oh, no, Lisa. We like having you here."

It was true. Lisa wore well. She was a bolsterer to Beany. It was solace to her spirit to have someone around who thought she was wonderful.

"But supposing a summer-school student wouldn't want to room with me?" Lisa asked.

66

"I was thinking about that," Beany said thoughtfully. "It might be easier to rent my little room. So if I can, I'll move in with you."

It was late Friday afternoon when Johnny gave a final dab in a far corner of the ceiling and descended the musical ladder. "With a little more practice, I could play 'Yankee Doodle' on it," he said.

The five gallons of paint wouldn't have been enough if they hadn't thinned it on the home stretch. The thinnest was behind the door.

The three stood and looked about the room. "I never knew bricks to be so pushy," Johnny said. For the red of the bricks still showed through both the coating of white and green paint. The two walls that Beany had visualized as oyster white, like the ones in Jennifer's rumpus room, were a mottled red and white, something like curdled cream and strawberries. The two that she had pictured the opaque and restful green of Jennifer's were a blotchy green, like nothing she had ever seen before.

"It'll all have to have another coat," she said wearily, as Johnny folded the ladder and reached for the can of paint remover for use on himself.

"The next coat will go on easier," Lisa encouraged. She giggled. "Johnny, your hair is all spotted with white."

"The boy with the polka-dotted hair," Johnny said. "Looks like I'm going to have to break down and get a haircut."

"You've needed one for weeks," Beany reminded him.

While he was scrubbing himself with smelly paint remover, Beany and Lisa dropped down on the floor, covered with rumpled newspapers, to clean the brushes.

Lisa said, "Beany, look! Here's a picture of Ty in this

67

old paper. And a write-up about his winning some baseball game."

Beany took the paper from her and glanced at the small headline on the sports page: TWIRLER TY BRINGS WIN TO TYSON HIGH.

She read aloud the paragraph under the heading:

> Ralph Tyson, pitching a game of shutout ball, won his home town second place in the Valley Prep League. If Tyson pitches his same airtight game two weeks from today when they meet their heftiest rival, Sun Ridge, the championship will be in the bag for Tyson High.

The small inset picture showed Ty in a baseball cap, squinting in the sun and smiling confidently.

Beany looked at the date on the old *Call*. It was March twenty-seventh. She said, "You know what would be fun? To cut out this picture and write-up and then present it with a real flowery speech to Ty when we have our ice cream tonight."

"He'll lap that up," Lisa said with a wry smile and went on sudsing the paint brushes in their murky liquid.

Johnny added soberly, "I wish Ty would get over his star-athlete complex and settle down and study. It'll take more than a pitcher's arm to get him into the U this fall."

"I keep wondering why he never gets any mail from Tyson," Beany said. "It's been over a week since he came and—"

"He gets his mail at the creamery," Johnny said. "He hears from his mother every few days. He says she keeps urging him to come home. I'm off. If the prof should call, tell him I had to stop at the barbershop."

But in only a few minutes he was back, to thrust at Beany

a sheaf of letters and cards. "The mail. In our absorbed labor underground, we forgot to bring it in."

With fingers that were sticky with paint, Beany sorted through it as Johnny raced up the basement steps. She turned over a post card of a mountain scene in Mexico and read her father's message: "Will write more later. Just now finished my column. Let's have a long letter from the home folks." And Adair had written on the blue sky over the mountains, "Glad you have a girl staying with you, Beany. She'll be company for you. Write us more about your boarders."

She would wait and write the long letter, Beany decided, after Miss Rutledge arrived, and after she had her other boarder. She took a happy moment of looking ahead to the time when she would lead her parents to the finished rumpus room in all its red-carpet and rattan-chaired splendor. "I can't believe it," an amazed Adair would say.

Another post card was from Beany's friend, Miggs Carmody. "All sorts of surprising things are happening on our trip," Miggs wrote. "Will wait and tell you and Johnny about them."

And I'll have a surprising something to show her, Beany thought.

"Oh, and here's a letter for you, Lisa."

Lisa looked startled. "For me?" She got up stiffly from her brush-cleaning. "I'll bet Father Hugh gave my folks this address. They needn't write and tell me to come home, because I won't."

"No, it's from Pfc. Jos. Kaswell at the marine base in San Diego. He's Andy Kern's buddy. I told Andy you made the cookies—you did, remember? So, because Andy says Kansas—that's what they call him—never got any mail, I

69

put his name on the box, too." Beany pulled off her scarf, extracted a hairpin from her braids. "Here, open it with this."

Lisa took the letter with fingers smeared with green paint. She opened it, ran dazed eyes over it.

"Did he like your cookies?" Beany prompted.

Lisa lifted rapt eyes. "It's the first time a boy ever wrote to me," she said breathlessly.

"I guess he must have liked your panocha bars," Beany prompted again.

"Oh yes. He said they were the best he ever ate—in all his life. Listen." Her eyes dropped to the letter and she read:

> Dear Lisa:
> I am writing to tell you that the cookies you made were the best I ever ate in my whole life. If you have time I would like to hear from you. And if it wouldn't make you mad for me to ask you, I would sure like you to send me your picture. All the other fellows have pictures of girls, but maybe you don't want to send your picture to a stranger, but I am not exactly a stranger because Andy and I know each other real well.
>
> Yours truly,
> Jos. Kaswell

"Sounds like a nice guy," Beany said. "I'll bet he'll be watching every mail for an answer from you."

Lisa folded the green-smudged letter, put it in the green-smudged envelope, and thrust it under the front of her blouse. (Only it wasn't a blouse, but a very old and ragged shirt of Johnny's, which she filled out more than Johnny ever had.)

She murmured again with a rapt smile, "It's the first

time a boy ever wrote to me. It's the first time a boy ever wanted me to write to him."

Beany shuffled through the rest of the mail. All ads and circulars. Funny, Andy hadn't written to thank her and praise the cookies. She'd probably hear tomorrow. She laid the mail on the stool, poured a palmful of paint remover in her hand, and attacked her hands and arms.

Lisa exclaimed, "Beany, what'll I do? He wants a picture of me. I just couldn't send him one. I'd never hear from him again."

"Well, I don't know," Beany said. Her matchmaking plans hadn't considered an exchange of pictures.

Lisa said with low emphasis, "I'm going to reduce. Right away, I'm going to."

An amazed Beany turned and looked at her. Lisa's round chin was set resolutely. "You are? But I thought you said that your being fat was glandular—and that it ran in the family."

Lisa flushed guiltily. "That's what Grandma always said, and I—I guess I just wanted to believe it. But it wasn't the truth, Beany. Nosir, I'm going on a diet, starting right this minute, and if I stick to it—and I will!—I can lose fourteen or sixteen pounds the first month."

"But don't you have to go to a doctor and have him make out a diet for you and all that?"

Again Lisa flushed deeply as she confessed, "Mother dragged me to a doctor last spring, right after Grandma died and I came home. And he gave me a diet. I know it all by heart." She reached for a cloth and dabbed at a stubborn spot of paint on Beany's cheek, as she went on, "I stayed on it long enough to lose seven pounds and then—then I didn't stay on it." She took the letter from its hiding place, fingered it again. "But this time I'll stick to it."

Beany saw the dedicated stubbornness in her eyes. "I'll bet you will," she said, and her enthusiasm rose. "And you can kind of stall Kansas along about your picture. You know—tell him that you didn't bring any with you, or that you're waiting to get film for your camera. Your letters will keep him happy for a while."

"You didn't tell Andy I was a fatty, did you?" Lisa asked anxiously.

Beany shook her head. "Oh, no. Gee, I wish Adair were here. She could do a sketch of you that'd be you *after* you took off a lot of pounds. Ug, my face feels stiff as a board with all that turpentiny stuff drying on it. I'm heading for the bathtub and hot soapy water. Want me to depaint you first?"

"No, you go on," Lisa said in a planning and faraway voice.

Beany was just drying her scrubbed self when the telephone rang. Her wet feet made tracks down the stairs and through the hall as she draped her terry-cloth robe about her.

It was Father Hugh calling from Twin Pine. "Beany, how would you folks like to gorge yourself on trout this evening? You never saw as beautiful a catch as I've got here for you. I was wondering if there was anyone there who could come up after them."

"I'll come a-runnin'," Beany said happily. "We've been painting, and we're all hollow as gourds and there's nothing much in the house to eat. I'll ask Lisa to come with me."

9

AND so again Beany set out for Twin Pine in Johnny's light blue car. She had asked Lisa to go with her, but Lisa had shaken her head. "You go, Beany. You ask Father Hugh if he called up the folks in Wichita and what they said. I'm afraid if I go he'll tell me I ought to go home."

"I'll tell him you ought to stay," Beany had said staunchly.

She turned off the boulevard and onto the highway. Whew-w, it was good to be on the road and out of that smelly basement. She hated to think about that extra outlay for paint for the second coat. She might even have to buy a new brush or two, for the bricks had worn down the bristles.

But next Monday there would be board money to put in the Sinking Fund. There would be a young teacher in Beany's own room. There would be the older Miss Rut-

73

ledge. Again she felt a surge of irritation. That nosy Judge Buell, doing her out of two nice men boarders.

But with a profit of over sixty dollars a month she could still squeeze out her rumpus room. Especially if one of the expected two were a small eater. None of the four now under the Malone roof could be called that. Not Johnny. Mary Fred always said, "It's beyond me, how any human can stow away food like Johnny, and *still* look like one of the underprivileged." Ty ate with an athlete's heartiness. And Lisa—

Oh, but Lisa would be on a reducing diet. She wouldn't be pouring half-and-half on breakfast food and constantly reaching for butter and jam for her toast. Funny, that a girl would run away from home because her family nagged at her to reduce, and then one letter from a Marine she had never seen would bring forth a determined, "I'm going to reduce!" Ah, romance.

Beany thought of Andy Kern. She wished he could come home on leave. But he had written that he wasn't due for one until late summer. It'd be fun to go dancing. She thought of Dulcie's saying that Ty had dropped right in her lap. It *would* break the monotony to go out to Acacia Gardens with him and dance to Benny Boden's orchestra.

She took the left turn off the highway that led up a hilly road to Twin Pine's stone rectory. Father Hugh opened the door for her. "Sit down and have a glass of lemonade, before I send you and the fish packing. You know the saying, 'The shorter the time between the stream and the skillet, the sweeter the fish.' I thought maybe Lisa would come with you."

"She's scared of you. She's afraid you'll send her packing back to Wichita. Did you telephone her folks?"

74

"Indeed, and I did." His voice took on a stronger brogue. "And I'm not so sold on her going back since I talked to them."

"What did they say?"

"It wasn't what they said. But it did seem to me they could have had more patience and forbearance with the child. Them and their talk about her not cooperating or trying to adjust. In fact," he admitted with a sheepish grin, "I'm afraid I lost my temper a bit. I told that sister of hers there were other ways of turning a wedding into a farce, besides having a fat sister standing beside her at the altar."

"Will they let her stay here?" Beany asked anxiously.

"I told them to let her alone, that she was happy where she was and there'd be little sense in dragging her back where she wasn't. Oh, don't get me wrong, Beany, they're not mean or hard-hearted at all. Maybe it was a mistake in the first place for poor Lisa to spend so much time with her grandmother, so that the family grew apart and there was much of this adjusting, that they talked about, on all sides."

"Who did you talk to besides her sister Jean?" Beany, the curious, asked.

"I talked to them all. The father's a very decent fellow. He's a traveling man, and away from home a good deal, and he said he had no idea Lisa was so unhappy. They flew off the handle about Lisa telling them this relative across from you was expecting her. She shouldn't have deceived them. Just because you feel sorry for her, Beany, don't think she's wholly blameless."

"I know," Beany admitted, sipping her lemonade. "But it was the only way she could think of to get away."

"I told them to bide their time, and they'd find Lisa

would be glad to come home of her own accord. It wouldn't surprise me, either, if the sister decides she wants her for a bridesmaid this fall," he ended, and went to get the trout from the refrigerator.

Beany called after him, "Lisa's going to reduce."

"Is she now!" he said, as he reappeared with the package of fish.

"She got a letter from a Marine friend of Andy Kern's—"

"I suppose you and Andy had a hand in that."

Beany laughed and explained about the cookies. "It was the first time she ever got a letter from a boy—and he wants her picture, so she decided right then and there that the pounds had to come off."

"Tell her as soon as she's thinner, I'll come in and take a fine picture of her to send her young man."

He had unwrapped his catch of fish to show her. He told about the scrap one large speckled trout gave him. And then he said, "Begone with you, you chatterbox. It'll be dusk now before you get home."

He walked out the door with her. "I've something to send Johnny, too. I was telling him about fool's gold that deceived so many by its glitter, when it was really nothing but pyrites. Here's a big chunk—I'll put it in your car."

They stood for a moment after Beany laid the wrapped fish on the front seat and he deposited the rock on the floor. The sun, in a splash of crimson, was setting behind the peaks. The mountain air was a little chill, and Beany wriggled into her sweater.

Father Hugh reached over and pulled her white collar outside it. "You look pretty in green. You're a pretty girl, Beany."

Maybe it was his words, or maybe it was the roseate glow

that bathed the world, but Beany drove homeward feeling gay and on top of the world. She wished she was going to a party.

Why not have a fish-fry party in the backyard when Ty came home from the creamery and Johnny from the TV station? Yessir, the minute she reached home, she'd phone Dulcie and Rosellen.

She thought of asking Jennifer Reed. No—no, she and Jennifer had never mixed socially. She had never been to Jennifer's house except to staff meetings. And besides, Jennifer always had everything so perfect. If only the Malones had better lighting for the yard. Johnny was always talking about rigging up a light over the back-porch door, but it was still in the offing.

She came to the detour off the new and wider road that was being built. She slowed almost to a stop to turn onto it. There, marking the turnoff, sat a row of lighted flares, their yellow tongues of flame fanning in the wind.

"It'd take a cyclone to blow one out," Ty had said. . . . Her eyes fastened on them. One was unlighted and sitting apart, close to the sign, "John Starr Construction Company," as though it weren't needed. Ty had also said, "Skip it. I just thought you weren't the father-ridden kind."

She laughed aloud, thinking of the triumph it would be if a black pot with an undaunted flame could be sitting on their outdoor table for the fish-fry tonight.

And why not? That unlighted one would never be missed. She had only to open her car door, step out, and snatch it up. She shot a swift glance around in the graying dusk. Not a road worker was in sight. Two cars passed her, throwing up a dust screen. There were no oncoming cars close enough to see her—

Almost without volition, she pulled on the brake, leaped

77

out, and grabbed up the unlighted pot. It was full of oil and heavier than she expected, and slippery and greasy with soot. She thrust it on the floor of the car. No, that wouldn't do, for it would roll over and spill out oil. Hurriedly, she took the heavy chunk of ore Father Hugh had given her and, with it, braced the pot against the outer door on her right.

She bent over to release the brake. It stuck a little, as it often did. Just as she loosened it, a car going toward the mountains passed her and honked. The driver slowed as best he could in the line of cars, motioned, and called something in passing.

It all happened so quickly while her eyes were on the brake. In the thinning dust and dusk, she couldn't see what kind of a car it was or who was in it.

A startled Beany drove on. Could it be one of the road crew who had seen her take the flare? That's what a guilty conscience did for you. It was probably just one of Johnny's friends who recognized Blue Monday and honked and waved in passing. But she drove toward town as fast as she dared, glancing back uneasily to see if she were being followed.

Finally she was off the highway and on the wide one-way street, off which she would turn onto College Boulevard. She relaxed in relief. It was only a few blocks then to Barberry Street and home.

She had edged over to the left lane to be ready for her turn when she heard the wail of a police siren behind her. Her heart lifted high and wild in her throat. She hugged close to the curb, praying that the police car would pass her, as it was passing all the other cars, without a glance.

But it didn't. It swished up close beside her on her right,

and this time there was no mistaking the peremptory signal to stop. There were two men in the car. The officer behind the wheel demanded, "Why didn't you stop back there on the highway when we motioned you down?"

Then she had been seen when she picked up the black pot!

In one flash she visualized the awful consequences. The *Tribune,* rival paper of the *Call* her father wrote for, would run headlines, "DAUGHTER OF WELL-KNOWN COLUMNIST ARRESTED FOR THEFT. BEANY MALONE OF HARKNESS HIGH AND EDITOR OF THE SCHOOL PAPER——" You wouldn't think you could live through so much in just the brief moment while you waited for what the policeman would say next. Even if the *Hark Ye* staff didn't *ask* her to resign, she'd have to. She'd be pointed out in halls. She could see the teachers looking at her sadly and thinking, "Beany Malone, of all people!" She could hear her father say, "Stealing is stealing, child."

The man next to the driver got out and came toward her. Beany stared at him. That wasn't a *police* uniform he wore. It was a khaki shirt that fitted snugly over his ribs. It was an overseas cap, with a rakish slant, on his head. He said, "Holy Smoke, Beany, what's the idea of giving us such a wild-goose chase?"

It was Andy Kern. Yet it wasn't the old easy-going Andy. He looked out-of-sorts and short-tempered. She lifted dazed eyes to the man at the wheel. It was Captain Kern, Andy's father.

Andy, too, demanded, "Didn't you see us when we passed you? We honked and yelled at you to wait."

Her words came out thinly, "I didn't—know it was—you." She managed to add, "You said you didn't have a—

a—" she couldn't even think of the word *leave*, "—vacation for a while."

This wasn't a regular leave, he explained. He and another Marine had been sent back on a plane to pick up a straggler. "A straggler is a guy who has gone AWOL." They would pick him up at the Lowry stockade in the morning and take him back to San Diego.

Beany could only sit there and stare at him in the half darkness, with her shaking foot on the brake and her shaking hands on the wheel. Even though his words came through her ringing ears, they didn't make sense.

"So my buddy and I have this one night on the town," Andy hurried on. "He's got a date, and I told him we'd meet them out at Acacia Gardens. I called up your house and Lisa said you'd gone to Twin Pine. I talked Dad into running me out so I could connect with you."

She couldn't think clearly. She couldn't think at all. Her mind was still too jolted by that terrifying moment when the police car had pulled up beside her. She glanced at Captain Kern's hawklike profile as he bent over to listen to the radio in the car. She had always been afraid of him. And here she was, within arm's distance from him, with a stolen black pot on the floor of her car.

Andy said with a flash of his old humor, "Where're your manners, girl? Aren't you going to take me in, so Dad can go on about his business of chasing down the lawbreakers? I had to pick out a girl with transportation, seein' as I'm afoot. I'm in the mood for dancing, and you look dressed up enough to go on to Acacia. I hear Benny Boden's playing out there. We leathernecks will even put out for a dinner, as long as it's a big night for us."

She should have said, "Oh, Andy, that sounds wonderful." It *was* wonderful. Andy Kern in town for an evening; a chance to go dancing at Acacia Gardens. Instead she said stupidly, "Father Hugh gave me some fish. I have to take them home."

"O.K., I'll go along with you." He made a move toward the door of her car to open it.

Instinctively she put her hand on the door to hold it shut. "No—no, you can't!" For if that door were opened, the black pot braced against it would go rolling out and land on his feet, and right in plain view of Captain Kern. "You see—I—well, I—" she fumbled.

"You what?" he flung out.

If only her ears weren't still ringing. If only she could think faster. But she could only flounder on, "I didn't know—I never dreamed you'd be coming—because you said in your letter—and there's something I have to do—"

"Something to do with that pretty-boy boarder Rosellen told me about?" he said coldly. "Absence makes the heart grow fonder—for somebody else, huh?"

Again Beany's eyes flicked to Captain Kern sitting there, immovable and waiting and within easy earshot. What could a girl say, or how could she say, "You get out of the picture, Captain Kern. I could make things all right with Andy if you weren't here." Why couldn't she be faster on her feet—like Dulcie Lungaarde or Mary Fred?

She tried to pitch her voice only for Andy's ears. "You see we have outdoor suppers and Ty plays the accordion and so I thought—"

Andy didn't lower his voice. "Is it yes or no? I don't have to roll over and beg to get a date."

Before Beany could answer, Captain Kern leaned out of the car to say impatiently, "If you aren't going on with

Beany, get back in the car, Andy. I've got a call to answer. I'll drop you off at home."

Andy waited for Beany to say something. But what could she say? He answered his father with a short laugh and a cocky swing of shoulders. "You don't need to take me home. Just drop me off at the nearest telephone, so I can get a date. I've only got one night in town, and I'm not the type to sit home and brood."

With that, he went around the car and climbed in beside his father and banged the door. The police car went zooming on, barely making the green light on the boulevard, as Beany watched with befuddled eyes.

Beany didn't make the light. She sat on. And, oddly enough, no sooner was the police car lost in boulevard traffic than her mind began to clear. Why hadn't she simply reached over and unpropped the black pot and pulled it over under her feet, so Andy could open the door without its falling out? Or, better yet, why couldn't she have slid over on the front seat and said, "Andy, go around and get in on the other side. You drive—you're a better driver than I am." That would have been a perfect way to protect the stolen flare from Captain Kern's sharp eyes. Oh, why hadn't she thought of that, instead of sitting there, like a stupid dope, holding the car door shut against Andy?

A car behind her honked, reminding her that the light had turned green. Jerkily, she moved onto the boulevard, moved on toward Barberry. She couldn't see, but she could smell the oily pot on the floor. Why had she been fool enough to take it in the first place? The stinking thing! Why hadn't she realized that she could never flaunt it on their outdoor table? Johnny would be the first to turn condemning eyes on her, to say, "Look, Beany, stealing is

82

stealing whether you take it from a construction company or out of someone's pocket."

A confused Beany drove into the Malone driveway. So Andy felt in the mood for dancing. He was even now on some telephone lining up a date for the evening—maybe he was on his way, for Andy would have no trouble getting a girl. He had always had his pick of the girls at Harkness.

And here was Beany Malone with a black pot she didn't want or know what to do with. She'd have to hide it someplace. She would be ashamed for Johnny—yes, or even Lisa—to know about it.

She got out of the car, tucked the fish package under one arm, and picked up the pot by the little ring that lay flat on its side. Her knees wobbled under her as she went in the side door of the house and, without turning on the basement light, hurried down the steps and into the wine room. She felt her way to the corner where they had left the empty paint buckets and thrust the black pot behind them. She even regrouped the buckets around it to hide it. It was the only place she could think of at the moment.

10

As Beany came up the basement steps and into the back hall, she heard Lisa calling from upstairs, "Beany, is that you?"

She walked into the front hall. "Yes, it's me—it's I," she corrected herself in a shaky voice.

"Are you alone?" Lisa called down in a near whisper.

"Yes, I'm alone." Yes, doggone it—alone, she thought dolefully.

Lisa came down the stairs, explaining, "I thought maybe Andy Kern would come home with you. And if he had, I was going to say I had a headache and stay in my room, because I didn't want him to see how fat I am and go back and tell Joe."

"Joe?"

"The Marine who wrote to me," Lisa explained in an amazed voice as though she couldn't imagine Beany's forgetting it.

"Oh, *Kansas*."

"Yes, you said Andy and the fellows called him Kansas. But I don't think folks ought to give people nicknames like that—you know, like my family and everyone calling me Pudgy. What about Andy Kern? He called here and I told him you'd gone to Twin Pine, and he said he'd start out and meet you. Didn't you see him?"

"Yes, I saw him," Beany admitted.

"Is he coming by later?"

Beany shook her head.

"He isn't! Why?" Lisa insisted.

Why? Why because Beany had stolen a highway flare. But she didn't want to confess that. "Oh, we got all fouled up. I was so scared when the police car came after me because I thought—well, Andy's dad, Captain Kern, was right there with him, just like a graven image. And the first thing I knew Andy was mad, and he told the captain to drop him off at a telephone so he could get a date—and he said he wasn't the kind to sit home and brood. . . ."

Her voice trailed off. It seemed even worse to lie to Lisa, because Lisa was so ready to believe, so unquestioning.

She took the package of fish which Beany still clutched. "Oh mercy, that's just too bad. Because Andy said this was a big night for him, and he was so anxious to get hold of you. I could hear him asking his dad to run him out toward Twin Pine, and I could tell his dad was pretty grumpy about it."

"He was even grumpier when he stopped me."

"Oh, Beany, I'll bet Andy didn't call up some other girl at all. He might even be home. Why don't you phone and see? I'll bet he'd be glad if you did."

Hope lifted in Beany. Maybe Andy hadn't found a girl,

85

available and eager—*and* with transportation to Acacia Gardens—on such short notice. She moved to the telephone and dialed the Kern number. If only Andy would answer!

But a clipped voice said, "Captain Kern speaking."

That threw Beany off guard and she stammered, "Oh, I didn't think . . . I thought maybe Andy would answer."

"He's out on a date."

Then he *had* found someone. She wanted to ask, Who with? But, of course, she didn't dare. Unwittingly, Andy's father supplied the information—or, at least, part of it. "Is this you, Sylvia?" and, perhaps taking her silence as assent, added in the somewhat disgusted voice of a parent having to mix in the social life of his children, "If he hasn't shown up yet, he will any minute. He said something about getting a shoeshine."

"Oh—well, thanks," Beany murmured and hung up.

"Was he there?" Lisa asked.

"No. He's on his way for his big night."

And he certainly hadn't let any grass grow under his feet either. He was in the mood for dancing, and it didn't matter to him whether he danced with Beany Malone or someone named Sylvia. Sylvia who? Beany knew several Sylvias. Maybe it was that red-headed one who had gone to Harkness High and then transferred to Huxley Hall, the expensive girls' school out beyond the university. *That* Sylvia could provide a car for a Marine who was afoot.

Andy hadn't even thanked her for the cookies she had sent—he hadn't even mentioned them.

She got up from the telephone with the sudden vigor of anger. "So that's that! Let's cook some of Father Hugh's trout. I'm starved."

It was Lisa who fried the trout, who set the table. Beany

moved about in aimless, haphazard fashion. It was Lisa who said, "Sit down now, Beany."

Lisa, already diet-conscious, removed the brown crispy skin off her fish and fed it to Red. She ate a salad without dressing, drank unsweetened iced tea.

No, Andy had lost no time in turning to someone else. Just because Beany had been so petrified with fear that she hadn't fallen into his arms with a joyous whoop. Even now he was probably turning his crinkly grin on this Sylvia person and handing her a dinner menu.

Lisa had to repeat her question twice. "What did Father Hugh say about calling my folks in Wichita—and did he say I ought to go home?"

The very anxiety in Lisa's face reproached Beany; and she thought, as she had before, that it was so easy to forget other people's troubles when you had troubles of your own.

"Yes, he called them." She picked her words carefully, not wanting to say anything that would widen the breach between Lisa and her family. "He told them you were happy here, and that he thought it'd be better for you to stay here for a while."

"Did you tell him I'm going to reduce?"

"Um-hmm, and he's going to take a fine picture of you when."

"I wouldn't let my folks know I'm going to reduce for anything," Lisa said. "I wouldn't give them the satisfaction—not after what Jeanie said about not wanting me in the wedding party."

"When did you say she was getting married?"

"Maybe September. It's something about her fiancé finishing some business in Hawaii."

"Father Hugh said it wouldn't surprise him if Jean wanted you to be her bridesmaid."

"Father Hugh doesn't know Jean," Lisa said with an unforgiving tightening of her lips.

They were still sitting at the table when the doorbell rang. Lisa exclaimed, "Oh mercy, Miss Rutledge! I forgot to tell you that she phoned after you left and said she'd be here later this evening."

"Wouldn't you know!" Beany muttered in irritation. "Why did she have to come tonight? I didn't think she'd be here until Sunday night or Monday. The room isn't even ready for her. Her and Judge Buell!"

The doorbell rang again. Beany went to the front door, pressing on the hall and porch light as she did.

At the door stood a thin, straight-shouldered woman with a large suitcase and a strapped package of books beside her. She said, "I'm Miss Rutledge."

"I'm Beany Malone. Come in." Her voice didn't even sound warm or hospitable to her own ears. But why had the boarder bobbed up when Beany was shaky and upset? "We didn't expect you so soon."

"Judge Buell asked me to come as soon as I could. He said he'd appreciate it."

He said *he'd* appreciate it, Beany thought irately.

In the hall, Beany saw that her new boarder was a prim, plainly dressed person in thick-lensed glasses; with the light glancing on them, Beany couldn't see the eyes behind them. She wore a summer suit of navy blue with a small white fleck like chalk dust in it. Chalk dust seemed to have sifted through her brown hair. Braids. Two thick braids were crossed atop Miss Rutledge's head, under her high-perched black hat.

That does it, Beany thought. My braids are coming off.

She rallied and said, "I'll carry your suitcase upstairs."

Miss Rutledge followed with the books.

And then Beany had her first taste of what it was like to turn a home into a boardinghouse. It seemed wrong, somehow, to take a stranger into the room so recently vacated by her parents. She grew even more resentful as the woman's eyes moved critically over the window seat under the corner window, the dressing table that was so completely Adair's, the leather chair that was so completely Beany's father's. She even wished Miss Rutledge would find fault with the room, so Beany would be rid of her.

But Miss Rutledge deposited her weighty books on the window seat.

Beany said, "I haven't had time to get it ready for you. I can take Adair's things off the vanity, and I'll move all the clothes into one closet." She couldn't help adding, "I planned to put two men in this room."

The new boarder answered stiffly, "I told Judge Buell I preferred to room alone. I'll pay ten dollars more than the usual rate. That was customary at the dorm where I stayed last summer."

"All right." That *would* help.

And then Beany had her first taste of what being a landlady was like. Miss Rutledge asked, "What time do you serve breakfast?"

"Why, we—we don't serve," Beany stammered. "I mean, we don't have any regular time. Our other boarder, Ty, just gets up in time for a nine-o'clock class."

Breakfast in the Malone household was never "served." It had always been a catch-as-catch-can affair, with the first one down putting on the coffee percolator; with the toaster sitting on the table; with each one reaching for his favorite breakfast food and looking up from the morning

Call to say to the one who was frying bacon, "Put in a couple of slices for me," or, "If you're cooking an egg, drop in an extra one."

Miss Rutledge said, "My schedule at the university calls for breakfast at seven-thirty, lunch at twelve-thirty, and dinner at six. I always believe in having these things understood at the start. It saves misunderstanding later."

She certainly was a "you keep your distance, and I'll keep mine" sort of person. "I'll have your breakfast at seven-thirty," Beany said. She didn't add that it would be a bit of a scramble, because Red, who was Beany's alarm clock, always wakened her at seven.

Miss Rutledge wanted to buy a *Literary Review*. Beany told her how to get to Downey's Drug, and she left Beany to turn the room into one befitting a boarder.

Grownups! How serene and cut-and-dried life was for them. Spending an evening with a *Literary Review*. What did Miss Rutledge know about an inner turmoil of guilt and anger and jealousy because of a rift with a boy in a Marine uniform? But then Miss Rutledge would never have done a fool thing like grabbing up a highway flare.

Beany crowded all Adair's perfumes and lotions into one drawer of the vanity. She shifted clothes so as to leave one closet for Miss Rutledge.

Clothes are such an intimate part of people. As Beany handled her father's robe and Adair's rumpled smock, with the sleeves still rolled up, an ache of longing flooded her. Boarders or no boarders, rumpus room or no rumpus room, she wished the summer were gone and it were the first of September, and that the yellow convertible, with Adair and Martie Malone in it, were turning into the Malone driveway.

90

11

THAT night owl of a Johnny! Would he never go to bed? Beany lay in her bed and waited for the house to quiet down. Because when everyone was asleep, she must slip stealthily down to the basement and find a new hiding place for the smelly black pot. She couldn't leave it in the wine room. Either Lisa or Johnny—or both—might go down there in the morning to see how the paint job looked.

She hadn't had a chance to do anything about it all evening, what with Lisa around, and then Ty and Johnny coming home at ten o'clock so hungry that she had fried each of them two of Father Hugh's trout.

And to think she had planned a gala fish-fry in the backyard not so many hours ago. She could have had it. It would have been all the more gala with Andy present. Then later they could have gone to Acacia Gardens. What a wonderful evening it could have been, if she hadn't been so rattled that she had bungled the whole meeting with him.

She hadn't presented or even mentioned Ty's write-up to him. She'd had too many other things on her mind.

There now, Johnny was running water in the bathroom. He'd surely go from there to his room—and to sleep. She hadn't even mentioned to him that Andy was in town. Johnny would have asked embarrassing questions about why Beany wasn't out with him.

No, she wouldn't think about Andy. She had said she was going to be a dollar-minded landlady this summer and by September have a rumpus room all her own.

If only this room of hers were big enough to crowd Lisa in, she could still take two more boarders. But there was barely space for her single bed, a narrow chest of drawers, and the vanity with the yellow, ruffled skirt she had made herself to match the yellow ruffled curtains. The room had never been meant for a room in itself, but for the nursery adjunct to the two-room suite Mary Fred occupied. It was after Beany's mother died that her father gave up the double room to the two older girls, Elizabeth and Mary Fred.

Now that Elizabeth was married and gone, Mary Fred was always saying, "For John's sake, Beany, why don't you move in with me and get out of that dinky little cubbyhole? I should think you'd have bruises all over from bumping into the bed or chest."

Yet Beany clung to her own little cubbyhole, because it was so all hers. It was at the head of the stairs, which gave her a feeling of keeping a finger on the pulse of the family. The door didn't shut tight, so that it was always to Beany that Red came when anything untoward happened in the night, always to Beany he came every morning at seven to nudge her to wakefulness. The Malones had never been able to figure out how Red knew when it was seven o'clock.

At last, Johnny was going to bed. She heard his door close, heard him and Ty talking briefly. She heard the creak of his bedsprings. She waited on in her dark room for complete silence. The clock in the hall struck twelve.

Her bare feet reached the rug by her bed. She didn't turn on a light but groped for her terry-cloth robe and eased out into the hall. . . . Oh dear, it did give the house a *boardinghouse* feel to it, to have Miss Rutledge there behind the door of her father's and Adair's room.

Beany crept softly down the stairs in her bare feet. She stumbled over Red, keeping vigil in the dark hall, and had to quiet his whimper of greeting; then she felt her way on through the hall and down the basement steps. She felt safe in turning on the light in the wine room.

Oh heavens! In her haste to plunk down the black pot and shove paint buckets around it, it had tipped over on its side. Pale amber oil had dribbled out over the rumpled papers that covered the cement floor. Lifting them up, she saw that the oil had penetrated the cement, darkening a wide area.

First she carried the offending pot into the furnace room. She put it in the farthest corner and hid it from view by placing the wide snow shovel in front of it. Back in the wine room, she gathered up all the oily papers and took them out to the ashpit. Ooo-oo, the grass felt cold and prickly on her bare feet.

With the stealth of a sneak thief, she hunted some old rags and went back to the basement and scoured up, as best

93

she could, all traces of the oil. It gave her an eerie feeling to be working furtively and alone, except for the watching Red, in the middle of the night in the quiet house. "Lady Beany Macbeth," she murmured to herself.

In the dark kitchen, she turned on a trickle of hot water and shook soap powder on her hands. The black grease clung. So did the oily smell. Like Lady Macbeth, she wondered if all the perfumes of Araby would wash the guilt from her hands.

The next morning a heavy-eyed Beany descended to the kitchen and connected the percolator and toaster.

Ty and Johnny would be sleeping late; Ty, because he had no classes, and Johnny, because he was always tired and relaxed after the Friday night program.

But Lisa came into the kitchen to help. She had written down her diet and she showed the chart to Beany. "This is the one the doctor made out for me. It's for two weeks, and then you start over. I remembered everything on it— the three-fourths cup of milk on breakfast food, the four ounces of fruit juice, the poached egg on pumpernickel toast. Only you can't have that *and* the breakfast food the same morning."

Miss Rutledge seemed every bit as unbending by daylight as she had the night before. She sat at the dining table and waited for her breakfast to be "served." Beany asked her how she liked her eggs, and she replied, "One three-minute egg, please."

Beany had to delve through drawers to find their egg timer.

After breakfast Miss Rutledge dressed to go to the university. She pressed her dress in the butler's pantry. Beany had always heard that men boarders kept themselves from being underfoot. If she could have had the two she expected to put in the front room upstairs, they wouldn't be pressing dresses every time they went someplace.

The teacher showed her first trace of indecision when she tried on a hat with flat white roses on the brim. She said, "I'm afraid they look too fussy on me. Maybe I should take them off."

"Oh, no!" Beany said impulsively. "They look pretty. You look prettier in that hat than in the plain one you wore last night. And some chalk-white jewelry would look nice with your dark suit."

Miss Rutledge gave her an odd look. "I've never paid much attention to clothes," she murmured. She added that she would not be home for lunch. She would go to the library when she had finished at the registrar's office.

Lisa came up from the basement wine room to announce, "The walls are perfectly dry, Beany. If you get the paint for the second coat, I'll start on them right away." She gave a rueful giggle. "Exercise will help me to reduce and keep me from thinking about how hollow I am."

"Are you awfully hollow?"

"Not as hollow as I will be before lunchtime. But I don't mind. I decided that when I think I can't stand it, I'll write a letter to Joe."

What Lisa was really saying was that you could stand a hollow stomach better than a hollow heart.

This summer I'm a landlady, Beany had to remind herself. I can't waste time, rehashing that awful scene with Andy.

She called the Housing Office on the campus and asked

if any summer-school student desired a small room with a single bed.

No, there was no request for a single room. "You see," the woman on the telephone explained, "so many of our students are friends who come in from the same town and they like to live together." She was very sorry, but she had no one listed that she could send to Miss Malone on Barberry Street.

Beany sat on the three-legged telephone stool, making a few halfhearted scribbles on the telephone pad. In reality, she was taking up the cherry red carpeting from the floor of her dream room. It hurt to do it—it hurt. But twenty yards of red carpeting had to go.

She said aloud to Lisa, "Maybe I could get the same effect if we painted the cement floor red and put down a few of those tufted rugs. I just can't manage the red carpeting."

"That's too bad," Lisa sympathized. "But a painted floor would look nice, Beany."

Yes, but not as *soul*-warming as red carpet.

That afternoon Beany and Lisa drove to the super market on the boulevard. There, Beany made a rather jolting discovery. A reducing diet didn't reduce a food bill. Fresh fruit, low-calorie canned fruits. Watercress and broccoli and brussels sprouts. Chops, steaks, and calves' liver. No hamburger. It had to be "lean, ground beef," which was twice as expensive. Cheap and filling items were not on a reducing diet.

Lisa realized it too, and she burst out, "Beany, I'm not paying you enough board. I'm going to pay you more."

"But you do more work around the house than I do. I couldn't charge you as much as Miss Rutledge pays."

Lisa laughed ruefully. "My hundred dollars wouldn't last long if you did. But I'm going to figure how much extra all these thinning foods are and pay you," she said stoutly. "What's more, I don't need brussels sprouts and broccoli. I can eat cabbage."

They reached home to find Ty just leaving for the creamery and Johnny sprinkling the lawn, after setting the hose on Mrs. Fletcher's across the street.

Miss Rutledge came through the gate with another stack of books in her arms. Johnny thrust the hose nozzle into Beany's hand, and hurried to relieve her of their weight. Wouldn't you know, Beany thought with something of envy, Johnny wouldn't find the new boarder standoffish or ramrod-stiff? He was asking her about her courses and what she planned to write her thesis on. He told her she was welcome to use his typewriter for her term papers.

It was Miss Rutledge who seemed to feel ill at ease under Johnny's friendly interest, who edged up the porch steps, saying that she had some reading to do.

12

NOR was Johnny impressed by Miss Rutledge's meal schedule. The next morning, which was Sunday, he and Beany slept later than usual; they came downstairs to find their boarder waiting for her breakfast.

"No seven-thirty breakfast on Sunday," Johnny told her. "You can have early coffee to hold you till we get back from Mass, and then you'll be treated to one of my legendary waffle breakfasts."

The Malones baked waffles not on an electric iron but an old black one—which was indeed iron—that baked waffles with a star in the middle, surrounded by hearts, and beautifully smoked up the house. But the very smoke, as well as Johnny's beating of egg whites, his melting of butter, all seemed part of a Malone Sunday.

So Miss Rutledge sat at the kitchen table with the four young folks on Sunday morning. The kitchen table, because Johnny insisted his customers should be only one whisk away from the stove.

Johnny had his own timing formula for baking them. He spooned the batter onto the iron, recited slowly,

"One, two, three, four, five, six, seven.
 All good children go to heaven,"

and flipped the iron. The next couplet went,

"When they get there they will say,
 'Where're all dem harps we're supposed to play?' "

But Johnny had a lot of variations and ad-libbing to the verse, such as he chanted this morning,

"Miss Rutledge cried with an anguished air,
 'I skinned my shin on the golden stair.' "

That goofy Johnny! Didn't he know that Miss Rutledge was their Judge Buell-appointed chaperone? She soon excused herself and went to her room and her books.

Johnny said, "I believe the woman's scared of us."

The calorie-conscious Lisa ate only half of a waffle. The previous Sunday she had kept right up with Johnny and Ty.

The young people were still at the breakfast table when a long distance call came from the senior Malones in Mexico. They said they had timed it so as to smell Johnny's waffles. Beany and Johnny took turns talking to them. Adair said to Beany, "We worry about you orphans."

"Oh, don't. I'm busy as that one-armed waiter with the hives."

"But, honey, this keeping boarders. What is it you want so hard that you'd spend a whole summer cooking and dishwashing and—?"

"Lisa's a lot of help. And the what I want so hard—well, that's a surprise. For when you come home in September."

99

Martie Malone asked Johnny if he'd seen his first "profile" in the Sunday *Call*.

"No, by gosh. We didn't think you'd have one in this soon."

"Clip it out and mail it to us. Adair's anxious to see how her illustration shows up."

They spread the big Sunday edition of the *Call* on the kitchen table. They read every line of their father's column, which was about the most famous bullfighter in Mexico. They admired the swing and action of Adair's accompanying sketch. "Just like *The New Yorker*," Johnny exulted.

"Imagine me in a nest of intellectuals," Ty said, and grinned across the table at Beany. "A writer father, artist mother, and Johnny, the historian."

She said, "For over a year I helped on a newspaper column. Some day I hope to be a columnist myself." The minute she said it, she realized she was saying the equivalent of, "Just look at me!" How sappy could a girl get? Just because she'd had a fight with Andy Kern, she needn't go overboard in trying to impress Ty.

"All I ever read is the sports page and the funnies." He got to his feet in that restless way of his. "How about us all gathering up the funnies and putting on our swim togs and going over to the park?"

Lisa shook her head. Johnny said, "Sunday's my day to take over the kitchen. You and Beany take the car and go. Ty, how about that book you have to read and write a report on for school? You'd better take it along."

Ty evaded, "I'll take it to work with me. On a cloudy day like this it's always quiet at the creamery."

As Beany went through the hall she saw the newspaper

write-up about "Twirler Ty," and she thrust it into the pocket of the terry-cloth robe she was taking with her.

A cloudy day with gray skies and a gentle feel of mist in the air. The kind of a day when Beany didn't have to worry about freckles popping out. She sat on a blanket on the beach, which was less crowded than on a sunny day, and read funnies and visited with Ty.

It was the first time they had ever been alone together. Dulcie was right. She, Beany, was lucky to have someone like Ty drop into her lap. Andy Kern needn't have been so callous. It was his, "I'm not the type to sit home and brood," that rankled so. Somehow, it would relieve the sting if Ty would show her a little attention.

She chattered on about Lisa and her pen pal in San Diego, and her slimming regime.

"Lisa, the giant economy size," he commented tritely.

Beany talked about Miss Rutledge and Judge Buell's selecting her for a chaperone, and Ty chanted out, "You can have her—I don't want her—she's too prim for me."

They sat on with only the rustle of turning pages, and a low chuckle from Ty as he read the funnies. Beany said suddenly, "Ty, there's Jennifer Reed. Over there with the tall fellow on a white beach robe. See, in the white swim suit."

Jennifer's beach jacket and shoes were also white.

"The snow queen," Ty muttered.

Beany suddenly wished she had bought a white suit, instead of this bright blue, flecked with gold. Among all the greens and reds and yellows, with their polka-dots and stripes, Jennifer's white stood out. It was like that at Harkness High, Beany remembered. Except that there, with other girls in colored sweaters, and checked or plaid skirts, Jennifer wore black tailored skirts with matching black sweaters of soft wool, with her only ornament a string of pearls—and not large ones either.

"She's wonderful," Beany murmured in admiration. "She has just moved into the loveliest pink Spanish-type house in Harmony Heights. And soon as everything is settled, she's going to have a party."

"Honoring you, I hear."

"I wonder what her new rumpus room will be like. Johnny thinks—and so does Dulcie—that I'm crazy to be fixing up one in our basement like Jennifer's."

Ty turned the last page of the comics and smiled at her and again wisecracked, "Anything she can do, you can do better."

Funny! Ty always made an apt and glib remark. As though they were right there, ready to reach for without even thinking.

Andy Kern wasn't like that. You could always talk things over with him. Could she swallow her hurt pride and write and explain to him why she had held the car door shut when he reached out to open it?

The air grew more chill. Only the hardy ones were going in the water. They came out blue and shivery with no sun to warm them. Beany decided *not* to go in.

She reached behind her for her robe and pulled it on. She thrust her hands in the pockets and felt the little square of newspaper, and pulled it out, smoothed it, and handed it to Ty. "Here is something for you to paste in your scrapbook and show your grandchildren in years to come."

He looked at it, then up at Beany and demanded, "Where'd you get that?"

"In an old newspaper. We had them spread out on the

wine room floor when we painted. It was only by a miracle that you didn't come out with green eyes or a green mustache."

He didn't seem to hear her. She couldn't read the expression on his face. He reached for his cigarettes, lit one with jerky movements, and flipped away the match.

Could it be that the picture made him homesick for Tyson? Beany said, "I guess you miss Tyson and all the folks and all the good times you had there."

He gave a grunting laugh. "Yeh, I miss all that—just like a dog misses fleas."

Beany pursued, "But Tyson's a pretty nice little town, isn't it?"

"*Was*, not is. Not since the school principal set himself up as a dictator and runs the town."

"I shouldn't think the people down there would stand for it."

Again that ironic snort. "They eat out of his hand. They think he's St. Peter himself. Even my own mother—she works in the school library, you know." He ground out the partially smoked cigarette in the sand. "Well, here's one he couldn't crack the whip over. Nobody's telling me where I can go and where I can't—or who I can buy a coke for at the drugstore, and who I can't."

He jerked upright, his eyes on the gray lake riffling in the wind. Beany had a feeling he was far away. He repeated with low vehemence, "Father-ridden! Rules! It sure burns me to a crisp the way some girls are like sheep, and never think anything out on their own."

Beany squirmed. It would never do to tell Ty that she wished she had been a little more father-ridden on that trip down from Twin Pine. She fumbled out, "But, Ty,

103

you can make a lot of trouble for yourself—I mean, it isn't being like sheep—I know it sounds like Sunday-school, but if you're brought up a certain way—"

Listen to who's talking, she thought ironically.

He didn't answer, but stood up, suddenly taut and restless. "Think I'll try some dives," he muttered.

He didn't ask her if she wanted to go in the water or if she minded waiting for him. He strode off toward the diving board. A puzzled Beany watched him as he dived in, climbed out, dived in again and again. It seemed as though everything she said or did was wrong these days.

Jennifer Reed walked over to Beany and dropped down on an edge of the blanket, and said with her gentle half-smile, "You didn't have a scrap with your boy friend, did you?"

"Not intentionally. Why?"

"Oh, I was watching him, and he dives in and swims out like someone who was furious about something."

The two girls watched. There did seem some driven anger in the way the boy in the blue trunks hit the end of the board with a thump, the way he came up and lashed through the water.

Jennifer said, "Beany, your long-delayed party is going to have to be delayed again. And, in a way, your talented stepmother is to blame."

"Adair?"

"Yes, my mother saw her illustration in the paper this morning. And she suddenly decided she'd like to have a bullfight scene or two on the wall of our rumpus room. You know—or maybe you don't—how she can get so carried away with her decorating ideas. But it'll mean postponing the party till some artist does the walls."

Jennifer seemed so regretful that Beany assured her
104

heartily, "That's all right. We'll have that much longer to look forward to it."

Beany snuggled closer into her robe, for the wind was growing stronger and more chill. Jennifer's boy friend came hurrying out of the water, draped himself in a blanket and beckoned to her.

At last, Ty came running across the sand to Beany. He was short of breath and spent, but not shivering. He grinned a little sheepishly at her as he reached for a towel and scrubbed his wet blond hair. "Beany, you look frozen. How about a hot dog?"

"Oh, Ty, we'd better go home. I think Johnny's planned dinner before you go to work."

They talked in desultory snatches as they drove home. But the nice, warm intimacy was gone. Ty was in his faraway mood again.

Johnny, Beany, and their three boarders were at the dinner table when the side door banged open and a voice sang out, "Make the bed and light the light—I'll be coming home tonight. In fact, here I am."

It was Mary Fred Malone. In snug Levi's that showed off her slim hips and a bright red jacket that picked up the red in her tanned cheeks, she came in and plopped down her overnight bag.

There was all the hubbub of greetings and of introductions to Miss Rutledge, Lisa Hold, and Ralph Tyson; and Mary Fred's saying, "Beany wrote me she was taking in boarders, so I had to come down and look you over," and Johnny interrupting with, "What are you doing down here away from the dudes and horses? Did you get fired?"

"Sir! I got promoted. Just look out in the driveway at the ritzy Lazy J ranchwagon I drove down. I'm the new meeter and greeter."

"Who are you meeting and greeting?" Beany asked.

"I'm to meet the plane from Dallas in the morning and whisk some moneyed guests up to the ranch. Service, for the millionaires who are above going downtown to the bus depot and taking a bus to the ranch. So you'll be seeing more of me this summer than you thought, because I'll be bobbing in and out. Aren't you thrilled?"

"Just frilled frough and frough," Ty answered readily.

And even as Beany was thinking: Goodness, with Mary Fred bobbing in during the summer, it's a good thing I couldn't get another boarder, Mary Fred said, "Hey, Beaver, with all your boarders, I hope you aren't rooming and boarding me out of my own bed."

"She almost did," Johnny said. "All that saved you was that the Housing Office only had boarders in batches of two or three."

Lisa said, with a shy smile, "I'm sleeping in one of the beds on your porch. I hope you don't mind."

"Not a bit. I've been sharing quarters with the cook, the barmaid, and three poodles, all of which fight to sleep on the foot of my bed—the poodles, I mean."

Johnny pulled up a chair for her. Beany reheated the coffee. Talk fairly bubbled. Lisa was explaining why she was taking no dessert. Even Miss Rutledge seemed less prim and aloof. Ty was telling Mary Fred he hoped she'd be at hand when he brought home ice cream this evening, and what was her favorite kind.

"Lots," she answered.

Beany thought enviously, Why couldn't I have that wonderful warming-up effect on people? No wonder everyone always said, "It won't seem like a party without you, Mary Fred." No one ever said that to Beany.

With the addition of Mary Fred and her date, the gathering that late evening seemed very much like a party. Dulcie Lungaarde and Norbett came. Rosellen Kern and Sidney Peale came. Rosellen had phoned Beany earlier. "Ice-cream social tonight? I've got a half a cake I can bring. It would've been a whole one, only the juvenile delinquents found where I hid it." She was referring to her two younger brothers.

"A half a cake is better than none," Beany had said, while the thought raced through her: I hope Rosellen doesn't start asking questions about why Andy got mad at me.

But instead she had heard Rosellen say, "Wasn't it swell to have Andy back, even though it was such a flying trip? I gather the four of you must have closed up all the dance spots in town that night. We could hardly pry Andy out of bed the next morning when his Marine friend called for him."

"Oh!" was all Beany could say.

So it had been a big night for Andy! And Captain Kern was as close-mouthed in family affairs as he was about police matters.

The ice-cream social was held in the living room because of the misty chill outside. Over the noise of it, Johnny called up the stairs to Miss Rutledge, "Come on down and join us."

Miss Rutledge demurred, "I have a book I want to finish before I go to bed."

"You might as well come down," Johnny insisted. "We'll keep you from concentrating anyway. And besides, you're supposed to chaperone us and have a sobering effect."

107

Beany listening, marveled. She couldn't say things like that to Miss Rutledge. She marveled still more when Miss Rutledge joined them. Her sobering influence was felt by no one but Beany. Not even Lisa, who was laughing ruefully with Mary Fred over the teaspoon-sized serving of ice cream Lisa had allotted herself. Only Dulcie was in one of her bad moods, and she never hid her ill-humor any more than she did her high spirits.

Beany asked her, "Are you and Norbett warring again?"

"No," Dulcie snapped. "The boss and I are warring. But don't get me started."

When the last guest was gone, Mary Fred and Beany gathered up and washed the dishes. They hadn't let Lisa help. "Take your poor empty stomach to bed," Mary Fred said, "before you slip and eat the last piece of cake."

"The nicest thing about a party," she said later, as she undressed in Beany's room, "is the post-mortem afterward. So you took Lisa, the overweight duckling under your wing. She's got a lot of little German grandmother mannerisms, hasn't she? Her saying 'Oh mercy,' with her 'Oh' more of an 'Ach.' If I ever do another paper on overeating and overweight, I'll use her—only under another name— as an example of what incentive to be pretty and slim can do. That matchmaking of yours, pet, was positively inspired."

"And now I suppose Ty is due for a psychoanalysis," Beany said.

"He's almost too good-looking to be true. And a spoiled athlete who's always had things his own way. If Johnny thinks he can turn him into a student, he's crazy. But as long as your Andy is so many miles away, it'd help pass the summer for you if you had a nice innocent fling with the fair-haired boy."

108

But Beany hadn't made much progress with the fair-haired boy today. She evaded, "I'll be pretty busy this summer."

"Oh, Beaver, I wish you wouldn't go off so half-cocked on that basement room with its scrofulous walls."

"They won't be scrofulous when we get the next coat on," Beany defended.

Mary Fred sighed. "You're such a stubborn little coot. Jennifer Reed has a rumpus room, and you've got to have one just like it. Where's my hairbrush?"

There was something so relaxed about the shedding of clothes in Beany's small room—the pattering into the bathroom and coming back with the bitey clean taste of toothpaste in your mouth, the very creak of the bed-springs under Mary Fred's brushing of her hair. How many times on how many late nights after dates and parties, the younger sister and the elder had taken out their hearts and emptied them to each other!

Did Beany dare spill out about Andy's return and the smelly black pot that had kept her from a date with him? She longed to ask, "Should I write and explain to him? Just this afternoon, I thought I would, and then Rosellen told about the big night Andy had with a girl named Sylvia something."

Mary Fred said on a mixture of yawn and chuckle, "Dulcie was certainly her most prickly self tonight."

"She was mad at her boss. She didn't tell me why."

"She told me. We were talking about it because the Ragged Robin and the Lazy J have the same problem. The boss laced Dulcie down for not watching the trays closer, so the customers wouldn't make off with the salts and peppers." Mary Fred shook her head. "The swipers. The sticky-fingered."

Beany stiffened. Why did *that* subject have to come up? She shifted quickly to, "Didn't Rosellen look pretty tonight?"

"She's a duck," Mary Fred murmured, and returned to the subject. "I can understand how some poor devil would steal food if he was hungry or clothing to keep him or his family warm. But the guests at the Lazy J are wealthy. They don't need to swipe our ashtrays and beer steins. The steins are cute, with the Lazy J brand on them, and so under someone's coat or into someone's grip they go. The boss has a card file on all the guests, and you'd be surprised at how many have S.F.—meaning sticky-fingered—written after their names."

Thank heavens, Mary Fred wouldn't be going into the furnace room where a black pot sat behind a snow shovel. Beany Malone, S.F.

"Yessir, and the ones you'd least suspect are the ones who think it's cute," Mary Fred mused on. "Sometimes it's an eye-opener. There was a fellow from Philadelphia up there last week—he gave me quite a rush, and I was pretty dewy-eyed about him, too. But he came out to the corral to bid me a fond farewell and ask me would I write to him, and just about that time I noticed that he'd sneaked two beer steins into his fishing creel—"

"What'd you say?"

"I didn't say anything, but I was suddenly *un*enamored."

"A couple of beer steins wouldn't make or break the Lazy J," Beany defended.

Mary Fred got to her feet and stretched so mightily that the short top of her pajamas was stretched above her midriff. "I suppose it's because Dad always dinged it into us so

110

hard. Remember how he always said, 'Swiping a spoon in a restaurant is just the same as taking money out of the cash register'?"

"Yes, I remember," Beany said in a small voice.

No, she wouldn't mention reaching out and picking up the highway flare that belonged to the Starr Construction Company.

13

IT was Miss Rutledge's lunch that broke the day smack in two for Beany. It seemed to her she no sooner got a good start on the repainting of the basement walls than it was time to lay aside her brush and come upstairs to scrub up and prepare the sandwich, salad, iced tea, and dessert that was the menu Miss Rutledge requested.

Beany had even suggested to her, "Miss Rutledge, if you ate at the campus cafeteria it would save your walking home at noon. And I could deduct the cost of your lunches from your board."

The graying-haired teacher had looked a little startled. "No, Beany, you see, the students out there are so much younger—and there's so much noise and confusion—" She added lamely, "I've got into the habit of reading while I eat lunch."

And, all too often, no matter how carefully she planned,

Beany found that she or Lisa had to make a hurried trip to the boulevard for something they were out of. Today Lisa had gone for a jar of mayonnaise and cheese. If only Johnny didn't help himself so constantly to what he called, "nibbling food."

Lisa returned and plopped down the sack and said in what Johnny called her "hungry" voice, "It was just like running the gauntlet again. The ice-cream wagon was stopped at the corner and all the kids were buying milk nickels. And the Ragged Robin was barbecuing spareribs —um-mm—"

"Nothing smells so good as those smoky ribs," Beany agreed.

"Except the Do-nut Shop when they're frying dough-nuts," Lisa said.

It was the second week in July and three weeks since Lisa had announced so resolutely, "I'm going to reduce."

But saying it was one thing and doing it was another. Poor Lisa. Twice she had bought the ingredients and made cookies to send to Pfc. Jos. Kaswell in San Diego. Once she had managed not even to taste one. The other time she had broken down and tasted one—and had kept right on until she had eaten five.

Both times, as she had packed them, she had asked, "Beany, couldn't we put Andy's name on the box, too, and your name along with mine?"

Both times Beany had said unhappily, "No. No, Lisa." She even added, for the little comfort it gave her, "He never even thanked me for the last ones." And how did she know but what Sylvia whatever-her-name-was was sending him cookies now? If Andy had even sent a message through Kansas to Lisa for her—she had hoped he would. But there had been no overture from Andy, and each day, each week made it harder for Beany to make one to him.

In the three weeks' time Lisa had lost ten pounds. "It would have been twelve or thirteen if I hadn't broken over those times—you know, the peach cobbler and the pork chops," Lisa said.

In the three weeks' time, Lisa and Pfc. Jos. Kaswell had become steady correspondents. The letters were now going back and forth airmail and almost daily.

Yes, to say what you were going to do was one thing, and to do it was quite another. It had been easy enough for Beany to say, "I'm going to turn the wine room into a rumpus room." Who would have thought that just the painting of the walls and ceiling would be so long-drawn-out and wearisome—and costly?

They had made limping progress with the second coat. Neither Beany nor Lisa could reach the highest spots on the wall, even if they stood on top of the rickety ladder —and a precarious stand it was. Johnny's long reach was needed. But he had so little time these days. In his gathering of material for the TV programs, he had to track down old-timers and old journals. And, as July's days settled down to heat and dry winds, he had to give more time to Mrs. Fletcher's lawn and shrubs and flower beds.

Johnny had written her about Lisa's coming from Wichita to visit her. She wrote back to Lisa with much apology, and advised her to return to Wichita, and come back to visit her later. For she didn't see how she could leave Martha until after the baby arrived in August.

Lisa had heard from her mother, too. Her mother saw no reason for Lisa's staying on with "strangers," and she too urged her to come home.

Lisa's face had set in stubborn lines. "Strangers!" she

muttered. "As though I didn't feel like a stranger when I was home."

"Any more news about Jean's wedding?" Beany asked.

"No, she didn't even mention it."

Now Lisa watched hungrily as Beany sliced cheese and took out bacon for Miss Rutledge's toasted sandwich. Lisa's lunch menu today was chilled bouillon, a salad of fresh fruit and two tablespoons of cottage cheese.

"I lie awake at night," Lisa said, "and just dream of eating a dozen sugar-coated doughnuts at a clip."

When Beany lay awake these nights, she thought of two things. Of her quarrel with Andy, and of that black pot in the furnace room behind the snow shovel. Did anyone else in the house notice the odor of diesel oil that seeped up the stairs along with the paint smell? But what was she to do with the fool thing? She couldn't put it out for the trash collectors for all the world to see. She couldn't toss it in the ashpit, for when the ashpit was cleaned it would be brought to light. Of course, she could some dark night take it out and bury it, or even dump it in some vacant lot. Still—still, that wouldn't be restoring stolen property to the John Starr Company.

She had even said to Johnny one day, "You know those flares they use to mark roadblocks? Have you any idea what they cost?"

"Those black pots? I sure do," he said promptly, lifting his eyes from some old photographs, "because I know a fellow who's working with a road crew this summer, and he was telling me that it nearly drives him nuts, trying to keep enough of them to mark the hazards at night. He said they could start a job with a hundred, and maybe end up with a dozen. You'd wonder why anyone would want to make off with—"

115

"Did he say how much they cost?"

"Yeh, they cost the company about two bucks and a half. Why'd you ask?"

"Oh, I just wondered," she said vaguely. "Ty mentioned once that it'd be nice to have one for our outdoor suppers."

"Nah! They stink to high heaven." His eyes dropped to a picture of an early-day honky-tonk in a mining camp. He added absently, "Just give me time and I'll rig up a light over the back door."

In the kitchen, Beany and Lisa heard the click outside that meant the mailman had left mail in the box at the front gate. Lisa hurried to get it. She came in, reading the letter that had come from San Diego. She lifted her eyes from it. "He's still asking for a picture," she said with a nervous laugh.

A package had come from Beany's stepmother in Mexico. Beany left the luncheon preparations to open it. In it were two skirts. One was for Beany, and the other Adair had sent to Lisa. They were tiered fiesta skirts. Beany's was of green print, full and swirly, with row after row of ecru lace on it. On the other Adair had pinned a brief note: "Lisa, I hope this will be the right size. I had to guess."

Lisa's skirt was of purple print with a tiny gold flower in it. And each full, gathered tier was weighted with black and gold braid.

"I never had such a beautiful skirt before," Lisa said.

Of course, Adair's guess had been too small. For when Lisa tried it on, the belt lacked some four inches of meeting. Even the two zipper tracks didn't come close.

Rapt anticipation came into Lisa's round, flushed face. "I'll have my picture taken in this skirt to send to Joe, just

116

as soon as I can lose enough more pounds to fasten it."

"With a fiesta blouse to match," Beany planned with her. "One of these frilly, lacy, off-the-shoulder ones. It'll be just like frosting on a cake with that skirt."

Lisa's hands sought out her upper arms. "I've got to slim down my arms," she worried. "In a sleeveless blouse, they'd look like hams."

"They'll slim down," Beany assured her, as she hurried to light the broiler. Miss Rutledge had come in the front door.

That purple skirt was to be Lisa's measuring stick, her inspiration, her soul-stiffener. Again and again in the weeks that followed, she tried it on. She and Beany rejoiced when the button on the waistband edged a fraction of an inch closer to the buttonhole. Lisa lived for the day when the two would unite and she could have her picture taken for a Marine in San Diego.

Miss Rutledge was seated at the dining table and Beany was taking the toasted sandwich from the broiler when Dulcie Lungaarde came breezing into the house and out to the kitchen, and demanded, "Let's see how much you've shrunk, Lisa."

Lisa showed her how she could lap the waistband of her old skirt which was not full enough to be a full one, but too full to be a fitted one. Lisa showed her the new skirt from Mexico. "This is the one I'll have my picture taken in. Beany says I should have an off-the-shoulder blouse to go with it."

"I'll make it for you when you're ready," Dulcie promised. "Hey, you two, I've got Dad's pickup, and I stopped to take you with me—"

"We can't go anyplace," Beany said in a whisper, with

117

a nod toward the dining room, "till we serve our boarder her lunch. Her schedule calls for it at twelve-thirty."

"Gawp!" said Dulcie. "Wouldn't you know that an old fuddy-duddy like Judge Buell would foist a female fuddy-duddy off on you?"

Lisa carried the sandwich and salad to the dining room while Beany added ice cubes to the tea. Lisa came back to report in a whisper, "She's reading *Silas Marner*. Can you imagine anyone opening that, unless it was required reading?"

Beany chuckled. "I'll be reduced to *Silas Marner* if I don't have a date pretty soon. I wonder what the first symptoms of old maid's insanity are?"

"How about Troubadour Ty with his smoldering eyes?" Dulcie asked.

"They smolder and then they unsmolder," Beany confessed. "It's enough to make a girl lose all confidence in herself. There are times when he gives me what you might call a play. But other times, I just blend in with the furniture."

"Not pin-downable, huh?" Dulcie mused. "You mustn't have the right approach. Maybe he doesn't vibrate to the homebody type with a streak of flour on her cheek."

"He vibrates to her food," Lisa put in.

Dulcie asked in a stage whisper, "You don't have to give your boarder waitress service during lunch, do you?"

Beany shook her head, whispered back, "No, in fact she prefers to be alone. I'll take in her dessert and the pitcher of iced tea." The dessert was peach pie.

Lisa said in a mournful whisper, "All the calories in that—and look at how thin she is."

"Now come on," Dulcie urged. "Dad's working at Jennifer Reed's new house. He's putting a covering over a patio, and he called up and asked me to bring out his metal saw. So I thought it'd be fun if you two rode out with me and got a close-up of the pink house."

She added when they were outside and could talk in normal tones, "If Jennifer is home, maybe she'll ask us in. Of course, we'll bask in all its elegance when she has her party for you, Beany, but a preview would be fun."

In the Lungaarde pickup, the three drove out to Harmony Heights. Every house in this new division had its own individual elegance. The lawns were kept green by automatic sprinkler systems. They were clipped close with power mowers. In winter the sidewalks were kept clear of snow by automatic warming systems under them.

Dulcie's father, in workman's clothes, his ruddy face reddened to the shade of a Winesap apple, was waiting at the low curb in front of the Reed house.

Beany's eyes drank in the widespread, pink plaster house in all its lovely perfection of patios, breezeway, picture windows, and lacy white iron grillwork. Its great expanse of velvet lawn was guarded by hedges, broken by a lily pool and a winding flagstone walk.

No, Jennifer wasn't home, Dulcie's father told them over his shoulder as he hurried back to his job.

Beany couldn't explain her odd relief. Not that Jennifer would feel snobbish toward three visitors arriving in a pickup and in most informal attire. But, somehow, the house looked as though it were posing for a picture that would appear in color in one of the home and garden magazines.

"Kind of a crummy little dump, yes?" Dulcie grinned, as she backed the truck and turned around deftly.

Beany felt envy engulf her—envy as dark green as the two walls of her rumpus room. So Jennifer's mother was going to have bullfight scenes on the walls of the rumpus room in this house. Some people certainly came by a rumpus room without a turning of their hand. And some people had to serve a Miss Rutledge three meals by the clock to get money for one—and, even then, practically sink the Sinking Fund to cover its rough walls.

She sighed heavily. Even when Lisa said, "It doesn't look like a comfortable kind of a house," envy was a brackish taste in her very soul.

When Dulcie dropped the two girls off at home, the Lazy J ranchwagon was in the driveway. Mary Fred was down for more meeting and greeting.

She was in the bathroom, washing her hair. The suds that whitened it made her skin look browner, her eyes bluer.

"Did you have any lunch?" Beany asked.

"Sort of. I joined your Miss Rutledge and drank some of her iced tea and ate a piece of pie. Then I ran her back to the U in the Lazy J wagon. Poor old soul."

"Poor old soul?" Beany and Lisa, amazed, echoed in unison, and Beany added, "What's poor old soul about her?"

"Help me rinse the back of my head, Beany." The spatter and swish of water, and then Mary Fred answered in a voice half-muffled in a towel, "Oh, life has kind of passed her by. I was asking her about her family. Trot out the bobby pins, Beany. Her father was an invalid for years and years, so she never had any parties or beaus— nothing but years of teaching third and fourth grades. No wonder she's made a shell out of a schoolroom and books."

Beany winked at Lisa, "So spake the psychologist of the Malones." And to Mary Fred, "You staying overnight?"

"Not this trip. I'm meeting some Bostonians on the seven o'clock plane. Don't hand *me* the bobby pins, Sis. Why do you suppose I waited till I came home to wash my hair? Because you can make such neat little snails, and mine always look like boll weevils."

She perched on the edge of the tub and Beany reached for the comb and started to work. Apropos of nothing, she burst out as she turned a wet strand of hair around her forefinger, "I haven't had a date since school was out."

"Goll*ee!*" Mary Fred said in a tragic voice. "You'd better start humping. That was hard luck for Andy to join the Marines, and for that nice Hank from the School of Mines to trot off for a summer of rock hunting. What's the matter with Ty?"

"What's the matter with *me?*" Beany retorted. "I don't seem to be the desirable type."

"Tut-tut! Make yourself desirable. Course I wouldn't say Ty was anyone to tie to—no pun intended, that's just cowboy talk—but a summer romance would get you over the hump."

Dinner at the Malones that evening was close to the nice, intimate tableful Beany had visualized at the Malone boarding house. Ty ate with them. Mary Fred had told him she would drive him to the creamery if he could stay, and Ty said he could because the fellow he relieved owed him some time.

Miss Rutledge and Johnny talked about Restoration poets; she was writing a paper on them. Beany and Lisa brought out their fiesta skirts from Mexico to show them.

Mary Fred drove Ty to the creamery, returned to report to Beany, "I think I've softened him up for you. I told him how popular you were at Harkness. I told him what a swell dancer you are, and he sounded sort of wistful—he said he hadn't been to a dance since he left Tyson. So take over from there, and you'll soon have him eating out of your hand."

It was time for Mary Fred to leave for the airport and then on to the Lazy J with her guests. Beany walked out to the car with her.

Mary Fred was suddenly the scolding big sister, "Now, Beaver, you stop acting as though poor old Rutledge were a cross inflicted on you by fate and—"

"Judge Buell," Beany corrected.

"The trouble with you, is that your do-gooding instinct is only aroused by the obvious. You never look under the surface."

"Rutledge scares me."

"Maybe this houseful of hoodlums scares her. She told me today that she had been around eight- and nine-year-olds for so long she didn't feel at home with young people —older young people, that is."

"All right, I'll be kind to our bookish boarder in her shell," Beany said absently, for there was something else she wanted to talk to Mary Fred about.

As her sister slid in the car behind the wheel, Beany ventured, "Mary Fred, I've been thinking about the fellow who lifted the beer mugs with the Lazy J brand. Supposing he—well, supposing he just took them on the spur of the moment and, after he got them home, he sort of wished he hadn't taken them—but gee, what could he do about it?"

Mary Fred picked up Beany's wrist to look at the watch. She started the motor. "If his conscience bothers him enough, he could always send them back," she said. "Bye, hon, till the next time."

14

THE cherry red paint Beany stroked onto the floor of the wine room was beautiful. Such a glowing, cheerful red. She took special pleasure in covering that wide area of cement that was darkened by crude oil from an over-turned flare.

But no sooner was the paint off the brush and onto the floor than its bright shine was absorbed by the unfinished cement. The floor, too, must have a second coat.

"We'll put it on tomorrow," Beany said to Lisa, as they both got stiffly to their feet. "And then it *will* look almost like a red carpet."

The red paint was supposed to dry in four hours. It said so on the can. And the next morning when they went down, the floor was dry and ready for the next coat except for the part where the oil had soaked in. It showed no signs of drying. You wouldn't think paint would have such a decided allergy to oil-soaked cement.

Day after day they went down and put a testing finger on it. Each time the finger came off smeared with red.

A puzzled Lisa said, "I can't understand why this part stays so wet and sticky."

Beany understood, but she squared her jaw and said, "With the hot wind blowing in the windows, it'll dry if we give it time."

But how much time?

It was still "tacky" when Beany turned the kitchen calendar to August.

August already, Beany thought in something of panic, and her rumpus room not wholly painted. In a desperate urge of making some headway on furnishing it, she took money out of the oatmeal box and bought one of the four small red rugs she would need, and one rattan tub chair of the twelve she had first pictured there. She might be able to do with six or eight, by bringing down an old couch from the attic and re-covering it.

August already, and Beany hadn't, as Dulcie said, set Ty's heart fluttering. She didn't, as Mary Fred put it, have him eating out of her hand.

They still held ice-cream socials of a late evening. Sometimes Rosellen and Sidney came over; sometimes Dulcie and Norbett. Ty still played his accordion while they sang songs about dreaming of you the whole night through. Sometimes, as Beany sang, she would glance at Ty's silhouette in the dark and ask herself, Why doesn't he ever ask me for a date? Why doesn't he ever say, "Come and go swimming with me, Beany?" instead of "How about us all going to the park?" As though Beany Malone had buck teeth or bowlegs.

She remembered back to her first dates with Norbett,

and how her making him peppermint-stick ice cream had pleased him so. And there was the School of Mines senior who had warmed to her when she washed the mud off his white shirt. "I'm putting Beany Malone at the top of my list," he had said. Andy Kern, too. Sitting in the kitchen after a movie, he would say, "I used to go for the pulse-beats, but now I'll take Beany with her fryin' arm."

Maybe Dulcie was right. Maybe Ty didn't vibrate to the homebody with a streak of flour—or paint—on her cheek. If only he could see her partied up. He had all the earmarks of a good dancer. If only Beany had a chance to show him she was easy to dance with.

She even hinted to him, one side of her deriding herself for it. "Dulcie tells me Benny Boden is wowing them out at Acacia."

"I'll bet." And then almost moodily, "It seems like a million years since I've danced."

"Maybe you could get a night off from the creamery and go," she suggested.

"Naw, this is ice-cream weather, and the boss is afraid he'll miss out on a few nickels if he lets anyone off."

"They go late to Acacia," she made further suggestion. "You know how Dulcie comes hurrying over here from the Ragged Robin and dresses and goes out."

He only muttered that he was getting pretty fed up with his creamery job.

What else could a girl say?

Another evening she said to him, "I'm going to get my braids cut off. Andy Kern always said, 'Beany without braids would be like a hot dog without mustard,' but don't you think I ought to get sheared?"

He laughed as his eyes rested on her. "Come to think

of it, the only female I ever knew with braids, besides you and Miss Rutledge, was a Mrs. Snodgrass who ran the bakery at Tyson. She was an old penny pincher."

Maybe, without his knowing it, he had a phobia about braids. Maybe his unconscious mind connected her with that penny-pinching bakery woman of his childhood.

Lisa was lighter by fourteen pounds, fifteen, sixteen— The button on the fiesta skirt with the gold flowers and braid was creeping closer and closer to the buttonhole. The zipper almost came together. Seldom a day passed without an airmail letter from San Diego for her. Seldom a day passed that Lisa didn't send one.

No letters came from San Diego for Beany. And she sent none.

Mail poured in from the goers-away to the stayers-at-home. Miggs Carmody wrote, "I can hardly wait to see your surprise." Letters came from their parents, as well as long distance calls on Sunday morning.

Again and again after work, Dulcie hurried up to Beany's room to change out of her carhop outfit into a dance dress for a date at Acacia Gardens. A kitchen-weary, meal-weary Beany would watch enviously. How long since she had sprayed perfume on herself!

"Norbett will sulk about my going out with somebody else," Dulcie would say, as she penciled her eyebrows and darkened her lashes, "but I think he enjoys it. So I might as well give him something to sulk about." Dulcie zipped up her dress, which was a lovely froth of white tulle and black lace bodice, and swayed to imaginary music. "That orchestra out there is heaven to dance to."

"I know," Beany would murmur.

Her unleavened spirits lifted when she received a telephone call from Kay Maffley, who had been her best friend at Harkness High before Kay moved to Utah last March. Kay was at the airport between planes on a vacation flight to Yellowstone Park.

"Beany, can't you throw a few things in a bag and go with me? We've got a cabin there, and Mother said she'd be so glad to have you along to keep me out of her hair— those day-long bridge games of hers—that we'd get your plane ticket."

"Oh, Kay, I'd love it," Beany said on a wail. "But I can't —not when I've got boarders."

She and Kay settled for a late lunch at the airport, and Beany drove out in Johnny's car.

Kay, with her taffy-colored hair and gentle smile, had been not only Beany's bosom friend but Johnny's girl before she moved away. She and Beany sat at the table and talked so fast they hardly knew they were eating deviled crab and tomato aspic. They shrieked gleefully over certain remembrances, turned sober over others.

Kay said, with her soft laugh, "Remember how I always envied you, how I used to say, 'Something's always happening at the Malones'?"

"Nothing very juicy this summer," Beany said with a twisted smile. "I'm fixing up a rumpus room, and don't you dare say, 'What do you want with a rumpus room?'"

"I won't say it."

Kay asked about Johnny with a fond, lingering smile. "Is he crazy about his new girl, Miggs Carmody? Does he miss her while she's gone this summer?"

"Oh, you know that crazy Johnny. He's no passionate Romeo."

Kay defended him, "Right now, he's too much in love

with the whole world to fall for any girl. Just give him time. . . . Oh, Beany, at first when we went to Utah, I was so miserable, so lonely for you and Johnny. But then—well, you know how life is. I started dating. The fellows gave me quite a rush because I was a new girl."

"And worth rushing besides," Beany interrupted.

"But I guess I'll always be glad that Johnny was my first boy friend—my first love. Because he's sort of a measuring stick—not that I'm looking for someone just *like* him. It's like Mary Fred always said, 'You are a different *you* as you go through life.' Or does that make sense?"

Beany chortled. "Um-hmm. Only I use my first boy friend, Norbett, as a measuring stick in reverse. I'm such a different me, now, that I keep looking for boys that aren't like him."

"You two had a rough go of it." Kay shook her head. "The battles I had to nurse you through. Isn't it nice to have an Andy in the offing that isn't the fighting kind?"

Beany said in a small voice, "We had a fight. Kay, there must be something the matter with me—or something *about* me that boys don't like. You aren't always fighting, Mary Fred isn't—"

"You and Andy had a fight. I can't believe it. What about?"

And then the secret that Beany had guarded from everyone else, she spilled out to Kay between gulps of iced tea—to Kay, who had always been her sounding board, her solace.

Kay was now. She said in gentle reproach, "Why, Beany Malone, my sympathies are all with Andy. He asked you to go out with him first, and you gave him what he thought was a brush-off. Why wouldn't he—when it was

128

his big night—go out with a Sylvia or a Gloria or anyone he could get?"

"I know," Beany mumbled, "but if just once he'd told Kansas to tell me hello—or something—"

"You're the one who should have written to him. Why in the world didn't you? And told him why you were so rattled and why you held the car door shut? That nice old Andy would have understood about your being so scared."

"It's too late now."

"No, it's not at all. It's never too late to say you're sorry. I can't bear to think of things being wrong between you and Andy."

Kay's plane was announced over the loud-speaker. Beany walked with her to the gate. They said good-by with tears in their eyes. Kay started to the plane, turned back to say, "The way we feel about each other—it's just the same, isn't it, Beany?"

"It'll always be," Beany said with crimping lips. "It'll always be as though we'd never been separated."

She watched the plane take off. Yes, it would always be the same. No matter how long between their visits, she and Kay would always pick up right where they left off.

She felt warmed and refreshed in spirit as she walked out to the row of parking meters and the light blue car. She was mentally framing a letter to Andy Kern—"I really wanted to go on a date with you that night, but I was afraid for you to open the car door because I stole a black pot and—"

129

15

JOHNNY was at the telephone in the hall when Beany returned. He looked up from his dialing of a number to say, "I'm trying to track down just a detail or two about the night the first train pulled into Denver—and having darn little luck. How was Kay?"

"Same old Kay. She asked about you," Beany said and walked into the kitchen.

No one answered Johnny's dialing, and he followed her out. "You know, Beaver, I was lucky to have someone like Kay for my first girl. I could have been a woman-hater, if I'd got a girl that made me cut my hair at frequent intervals and treated me with the disrespect I find at home—"

"Oh, hush, Johnny. Where's Lisa?" She wanted to ask her how long it took an airmail letter to reach San Diego.

"Up on the boul, mailing a letter. To friend Joe, natch."

On the kitchen table lay the unmistakable yellow and squarish folder that contained film or snapshots. "Whose pictures?" Beany asked idly.

"Oh those! Rosellen Kern called and said she'd been trying to get to Downey's Drug for them. Seems that Andy sends his roll of film to her, and she has two sets of snaps made, and sends one to him and keeps one herself. So I told her I'd pick them up and drop them off on my way to the library. And I'm on my way, soon as I change the hose on the Fletcher lawn."

He went out the side door.

Beany's eyes rested on the thick yellow folder. Pictures of Andy. She reached out to the yellow folder with its black print that said, "TRY KODACHROME." She laid it back on the table. She tried to put her mind on what a landlady should feed her boarders on a hot summer evening. Broiled chops and—and—

But there was nothing private about snapshots, was there? It wasn't like reading someone's letter. If Rosellen were here, she'd say, "Just look at these, Beany."

Her fingers reached out and picked up the packet of pictures.

The first picture showed Marines doing their washing; the next one hiking. And then Beany was staring at a picture of Andy leaning on a ship's rail with a blonde girl in dark glasses. The girl wore a short-sleeved sweater with flowers embroidered down the front. My, how chummy the two of them were, leaning against the rail, their arms touching. What wide, happy smiles they wore. Under them was the name of the ship, *Coronado*. It must be the ferry that ran between San Diego and Coronado Island. Andy had mentioned it once in one of his letters.

She dropped one of the slippery square negatives. She picked it up, thrust it along with the shapshots, back in the folder. She had seen enough of Andy's pictures.

"I'm not the kind to sit home and brood," Andy had

131

flung out that evening in June when they had met so suddenly and parted even more suddenly.

So why should Beany be the kind to sit home and brood, and send forth a letter of explanation and apology? A letter that meant the equivalent of, "I want to be your girl. In between the Sylvias and the blondes with dark glasses, please give a little thought to poor old Beany."

Hah! Any old day she'd write to him and eat humble pie.

She left the kitchen and slowly climbed the stairs to her room. The very stairs felt shaky under her. It wasn't exactly seeing Andy with another girl. It was just that that was the culmination, the final proof. She might as well face it. There *was* something the matter with her, some lack of feminine charm that other girls had—Mary Fred, Kay, Dulcie. They had dates aplenty; they weren't left stranded. She, Beany, was just a younger Miss Rutledge with life passing her by.

She dropped heavily down on the bed and kicked off her pumps. She ought to change out of her green plaid gingham and button herself into her pedal pushers and old striped blouse of Mary Fred's. And just what was she saving the green plaid gingham for? For sitting in her room and reading *Silas Marner*?

She heard Johnny and Ty talking on the front porch, and she felt vehement resentment toward Ty. Good old Beany, to fix him ham sandwiches, to hang his soggy towel and beach jacket on the line when he came in from swimming. She could understand now how homely, left-out women turned into men-haters.

And then she heard Dulcie's loud gaiety. The cocksure Dulcie was the one person Beany didn't want to see right now. Dulcie and her talk of dates would be rubbing salt in the wound. But Dulcie came bounding up the stairs.

She had been downtown shopping, and she had stopped to change into her carhop togs before going on duty at the Ragged Robin.

Beany listened to her and watched with dull eyes as Dulcie put on the short red skirt and frog-trimmed jacket. She slid her feet into the flared white boots, asked, "Got any white shoe polish handy?"

Beany got up and handed her a bottle, watched Dulcie swab it on. She asked, "How much longer is Rutledge-in-a-rut going to be on your neck?"

Beany said stiffly—strange, that she should feel suddenly defensive, "Summer school is eight weeks. That'll be about the middle of August. Rutledge is all right. She isn't as stiff and standoffish as she was, now that we know her better. I can understand perfectly why she draws away from life and buries herself in classes and books."

Dulcie was just saying, "Never mind the treatise," when someone rapped imperatively on the door, and called, "Beany! Hey, Beany, can you come out a minute?"

It was Ty, and Dulcie reached over and opened the door, said, "We're decent."

Ty turned his bright smile on Beany and reached out and caught both her hands. "Beany, I have to ask you something before I leave for work. I want you to go dancing with me out at Acacia Gardens tomorrow night."

Beany could only gape at him, wondering if she had rightly heard him. "You mean *all* of us?"

"No, for the love of Pat, I mean just you and me." Deep excitement was in his laugh, the gold flecks in his eyes danced with it. "I'm getting the evening off from the creamery. I've got to take you to Acacia and dance tomorrow night, if it's the last thing I ever do. Even if they fire me, I've got to go."

"You've *got* to go?" Beany repeated.

"I mean I've had all I can take of ladling out ice cream into cones for every kid in town and swabbing out the joint the last thing at night. I just asked Johnny, and he said we could take his car, and he'll ride down to the TV station with the prof. So let's make it a lark. You turn yourself into a party doll. I'll lay out for an orchid for you."

To go dancing at Acacia Gardens with Ty! And wear an orchid! Then he did find her desirable, after all. Then she wasn't doomed to have life pass her by. Somehow the sting of Andy and his having dates with other girls was less. Life suddenly had a bright and exciting lift.

"You will, won't you, Beany?" he pleaded. "I couldn't go to work until I knew for sure."

"Why, sure—sure, it sounds like fun," she said, trying to keep the squeak of pure joy and relief out of her voice.

The front screen door slammed behind Ty. She heard the front gate click. She turned to Dulcie and breathed, "Did you hear what he said? He wants me to go dancing with him tomorrow night at Acacia. He's going to get me an orchid."

"What're you going to wear under the orchid?" Dulcie wanted to know.

"Gee, what will I?" Beany answered out of her surprised trance. "I don't have one of those swanky sunback dresses that most of them wear out there. Last year when I went with Norbett I wore a lavender of Mary Fred's—but she took it with her. I guess I could wear that fiesta skirt Adair sent and a blouse."

134

"Nosir, you'll not go blousing and skirting out to the Acacia," Dulcie said firmly. "The times I've been out there, it's been very frou-frou."

"Well, I haven't anything frou-frou," Beany murmured.

Dulcie said musingly, "So the lad wants a party doll. Then, by cracky, we'll give him a party doll." She walked over to the closet and indicated her own white tulle and black lace formal that she had left there from her last dancing date, when she had changed her clothes at the Malones'. "You'll wear my dress. If it needs a stitch or two, I'll take them."

Beany's blue-gray eyes widened. "Oh, Dulcie, not your original—I mean, the one you copied from an original that cost $89.50."

When Dulcie, the swift and deft with a needle, had made that dress in their sewing class at school, it had been the envy of every girl. Dulcie had worn it as the grand finale in the spring style show, and a gasp of admiration had gone up from the audience. So gossamer, so lovely, with its fitted bodice of black lace and its white tulle skirt with an uneven border of black tulle, edged with cutout lace that Dulcie had whipped on by hand.

"You don't think I'd feel too dressed-up in it, do you?" Beany hazarded.

"I wore it twice to Acacia Gardens and I felt fine in it. In fact, every eye will turn toward you, Beany. Tomorrow night, eh? I'll get a half-hour off from the Robin and come over and see that you're turned out in proper style to set friend Ty back on his haunches. Just wait."

Beany found it hard to concentrate on getting dinner. As though broiling lamb chops mattered! It mattered so little that she burned her wrist when she reached into the broiler for the sizzling chops.

16

BEANY knew when she got up the next morning what she was going to do. The decision was already there and waiting for her. Her braids were coming off. Prim braids and that deliciously wicked dress of Dulcie's just didn't go together. Besides, she had a vague feeling that cutting off her braids would help sever all connection, all thought of Andy Kern.

Beany had had the final shove toward the beauty shop.

It was a new one on the boulevard, which catered to the wealthy clientele of Harmony Heights. Beany opened the glass door on which was lettered, "Adrian," and under it, "For a More Beautiful You."

In the pocket of her denim skirt was a ten-dollar bill. She had taken it from the Sinking Fund with only passing thought that it would buy a chair and pad for her rumpus room. She hadn't even heard the cautious part of her mind advising her: Now be sure to ask how much Adrian charges before you sit down in the chair. She was tired of counting pennies. Tired of sitting home and brooding. She was going dancing at Acacia for the first time this summer, and she was as fluttery as she had been in junior high over her first date.

She stepped inside the pink and silver salon with its artificial vines trailing out of wall vases. The three women operators were busy, so that it was Adrian himself who greeted her with a bow, a warm flash of brown eyes, and said in a French accent as though he were a mind reader, "You have come to get these—" he motioned above his own dark head, "—these cut off. Yes. It is right. You have outgrown them."

Beany said, "I'd like one of the new haircuts—maybe a sort of Grecian boy or—"

"No, no, no!" he said vehemently. "Nothing severe for so elfin a face. Short, yes, but veree soft. Daring, yes, but still an aureole. I know exactly the right shaping. You leave it to Adrian, yes? I will do it myself."

She had the feeling that he was bestowing a great honor.

She left it to Adrian for two hours. The braids came off. Scissors snipped. The white froth of soap, after which her head was covered with curlers. A long session under a drier. And then Adrian, rapt and absorbed as a true artist, wielding his comb and brush, while Beany watched with wide, excited eyes.

He did things with her bangs so that they were not the straight fringe she had worn. Now they were parted in the middle and given a rounded curl effect. The rest of her hair was a short feather-edged swirl that framed her face.

"There now, Mademoiselle. Truly, you are a more beautiful you, *n'est-ce pas?*"

"I like it," Beany smiled back and reached her hand up to her head. Truly, a different Beany. She got out of the chair, feeling lightheaded and lighthearted.

She gave Adrian the ten-dollar bill. It was too late now to haggle about price. He gave her back two dollars and some change. Even that didn't daunt her. This was a red-letter day for her. She was a butterfly emerging from—from whatever that drab thing was that a butterfly emerged from.

It was her first experience with the miraculous uplift of a beauty salon. She walked home, sure that everyone noticed her exceptional allure. She was even surprised when a neighbor passed and said hello and didn't notice that she was a more beautiful Beany.

She crossed the street to where Johnny and Lisa were trimming the Fletcher hedge. "Well, do you like it?"

"Whistle bait, no less," Johnny said, and Lisa stared in admiration. "You look like the girl who played Joan of Arc."

The rest of the day Beany watched the clock and stole glances at herself in the mirror. Miss Rutledge came home with her usual armful of books and notebooks. She asked Beany if it would be all right to use her father's encyclopedia in his study, and Beany said yes, quite all right. She added, "Did you notice my new haircut? I don't feel so weighted down without the braids."

Miss Rutledge smiled. "You're too young to be weighted down, Beany. The new hairdo is very becoming."

Beany felt a sudden warmth toward their boarder-chaperone. She said on a confidential burst, "Things have gone so wrong all these weeks, but tonight I'm going to a dance with Ty."

"You aren't—fond of Ty, are you?" Miss Rutledge asked, picking her words as though she were on unfamiliar ground.

"No, it isn't that. It's just that I haven't gone anyplace —and you get a feeling that you want *somebody* to think you're something. I guess that sounds crazy."

"No, it doesn't," Miss Rutledge said. "Not crazy at all. I know how you feel—I had years of feeling the same way." She laughed a dry, rueful laugh. "There's only one thing worse, Beany, than wanting to get out and go places, and that's reaching the point where you're afraid to."

And then, as though alarmed at her own lack of reticence, Miss Rutledge turned her attention to the open encyclopedia.

Ty came home at dinnertime. He was carrying not only a small square box from The Orchid Shop, which he presented to Beany with a flourish, but also a large gray box.

"I blew myself for our big flingding tonight," he said to Beany and Lisa as he unsnapped the string. He took out a white coat and shook it out. "I even had them press it." There was no hiding the nervous excitement in his eyes. "We're the upper crust tonight, Beany. By the way, it'll be all right, won't it, if I wait and catch up on my board on my next payday?"

"Yes, that'll be all right."

What else could a girl say to a boy who had just handed her a box in which a purple orchid nested? You couldn't carp if he had spent his board money on a white coat to take you dancing. She looked away from Lisa's eyes.

She didn't want to hear Lisa say, "But, Beany, the Sinking Fund is practically sunk." She hurried upstairs to start dressing.

Sure enough, Dulcie came banging through the front door just as Beany finished her bath. Dulcie brought her make-up kit, her bottle of Infatuation perfume, and a pair of huge, fan-shaped earrings.

She went to work, saying again with lip-smacking satisfaction, "If it's a party doll the lad wants, it's a party doll we'll give him."

Lisa came in and sat on the bed to watch. First Dulcie coated Beany's face and neck with a rosy tan liquid. "We can't have freckles spoiling the view," said Dulcie.

Then she took out her tiny metal box and brush. Beany demurred, "Oh but, Dulcie, I've never used eye make-up."

"There's a first for everything," said the imperturbable Dulcie.

Lisa said, "But Beany already has such dark eyelashes."

"No buts from the grandstand," Dulcie said, and wielded the blackish brush.

The dress went on next with Dulcie skillfully taking a stitch here and there. And then she noticed the burn on Beany's wrist. "Holy Hannah, how can you be a *femme fatale* with a housewifely burn on your wrist?"

"I could put a Band-Aid over it," Beany suggested.

Dulcie groaned at the suggestion. Her eyes brightened. "I've got it! And it'll be even ritzier than pinning the orchid on your shoulder, or as close as you can come to a shoulder with a strapless dress. We'll anchor the orchid on a ribbon and you can wear it on your wrist."

"Wear the orchid on my wrist?"

"Sure, stupe. Let me show you."

Beany made one more futile demurring when Dulcie reached for the earrings. "Gosh, Dulcie, those earrings are so—so—"

140

"So hit-you-in-the-eye. Right you are."

Perfume next. An extra touch-up of liquid on Beany's freckled nose. And when Dulcie finally said, "There now!" Beany stood and surveyed herself in the door-length mirror in the hall.

Dulcie's swift stitches had made the black lace bodice hug tightly. The liquid she had smoothed on with care blanketed every freckle. The shadowed eyes that looked back at Beany *did* have a look of seduction and mystery. She couldn't believe it. It was like that nursery rhyme, "Laws-a-massy-on-me, can this be I?"

"This is going to be one night," Dulcie exulted, "when every eye will turn your way, including those bouncy eyes of friend Ty's."

Friend Ty had evidently been chafing at the foot of the stairs during the dressing. He broke off his impatient, "Come on, Beany," to give a heartfelt whistle. "Well, I'm a monkey's uncle! You look like something right out of Hollywood." His eyes glowed his approval.

The Malone house on Barberry Street was on the south side of the city; Acacia Gardens was far over on the north side. With Beany beside him, all froth of skirt and sparkle of earrings and well doused with Infatuation, Ty drove Johnny's blue car across town.

They parked in the crowded parking lot inside the Gardens. On her high heels, with Ty's hand hurrying her, Beany teetered the distance between the graveled car lot and the bright lights, the noisy tempo of the amusement park. They passed in front of two yellow school buses with banners whipping on their sides.

And into the park proper. It had seemed fairyland to Beany as a child. It still did. Soft-colored lights overhead.

Hanging flower baskets, the smell of caramel popcorn. The lilting melody from the merry-go-round broken by the roar of the roller-coaster and the screams of its riders. Enchantment.

Past the theater, past the distorting mirrors, past the cotton-candy booth, Ty hurried her. Every eye did turn as Beany passed, and her pulses quickened in pure delight. Her head lifted, and she walked with an imitation of Dulcie's hippy swing.

Benny Boden's music reached out to them and fairly drew them to the pavilion. At the ticket window, Ty threw down a bill to pay for their admission, and only the faintest little whisper in Beany reminded her: That's part of his board money, too.

They danced off just as the hidden lights in the low ceiling shifted to a twilight pink. At first Beany gave all thought to catching on to Ty's exaggerated swinging step. She wished he wouldn't hold her so tight. And then her eyes began to wander through the twilight pink. It'd be fun to see some of the old Harkness crowd—fun to introduce the good-looking Ty to them.

Her eyes rested on two large banners over the orchestra stand. "WELCOME TYSON HIGH," one read. The other, "HAVE FUN, TYSON."

She said on a surprised breath, "Why, Ty, this is your hometown night here. That's what those buses were for. Remember, we passed them in the parking lot?"

"I know," he said, and though he smiled widely, the muscles in his jaw tightened. As did his grip on Beany.

Her eyes roamed over the dancers. All high-school age, and none of them "dressed up." The boys were in jeans and slacks with sport shirts. The girls wore bright-colored

142

cotton dresses or skirts and blouses. They looked mussed and rosy as though they had been outdoors all day.

Beany said, "I guess they all came up on a picnic and then the dance is the big windup."

"They do it every year in August. Supposed to be for the whole school, though it's mostly seniors and juniors. It's the big day, the big night for all the hicks that don't even know they're hicks."

Why hadn't Beany remembered? Most Friday nights at Acacia Gardens were given over to out-of-town schools, or a college fraternity, or a big reunion party. She remembered that the Harkness High alumni even held their reunions here on a certain Friday every summer.

So this was Tyson High night! Funny, Ty hadn't mentioned it.

The dance ended. He stood close to her, smiling down at her as they waited for another dance to start. It began almost immediately. The lights changed to lavender. Ty was unusually tall, and he held her too tightly. He danced jerkily; one minute going through fancy steps, and then slowing till he was out of step with the music. It was all she could do to follow him.

And then she realized that practically every one from Tyson was watching them as they danced. She had only to lift her eyes to meet curious, measuring ones that never left the girl in the black lace and white tulle, and the boy in the white coat.

A slow chill crept under her lace bodice. They were not friendly eyes. Was it because she was overdressed in Dulcie's black lace and white tulle and the earrings which suddenly seemed to Beany to be as widespread as peacocks' tails? She was sure the girls were nudging each other about the orchid on her wrist.

She longed suddenly to be in a full skirt and blouse and low heels. . . . A memory flashed through her mind. Once she had gone to a cocktail party in a penthouse and worn a blouse and skirt, only to find that other girls, other women were in "after-five" dresses. She had felt out of place then, but this . . . It was far more uncomfortable to be overdressed than underdressed, she realized in sick embarrassment.

She noticed, too, that the other couples were changing partners, that boys cut in on each other with friendly argument or a laughing scuffle. Beany pushed herself back from Ty—she wished he wouldn't hold her in such a vise—to say as they danced, "Ty, this is your old school crowd. You don't have to stick right with me. Go ahead and cut in."

His smile was too bright, too wide. "When I've got you, beautiful? Who could ask for anything more?" he chanted and tightened his hold.

An intermission was announced. One side of the dance floor was rimmed with small tables for serving refreshment. The dancers filtered off the floor toward them. Ty wasn't content to let her walk out beside him. He had to take her arm and hold her fondly close while he smiled intimately down at her.

There was a small jam at the exit from the dance floor. It seemed to Beany that Ty deliberately brushed against a slim girl in a square-necked, yellow cotton dress, that his, "Oh, hi there, Elaine," was deliberately casual. An odd, even hostile, tenseness stiffened the whole Tyson group.

The girl, Elaine, looked at Ty, then at Beany; and Beany felt the impact of the misery, the reproach, in her blue eyes. Her smile was forced and quavery as she said, "Oh hello, Ty." Just that.

17

Ty guided Beany to a table. All about them, other young folks were pushing two or three tables together and crowding around. Even though the other tables were too full for comfort, and there was room for more at the one with Beany and Ty, no one came near.

Again she asked, "Wouldn't you like to sit with some of your friends? Or ask some of them to sit with us?"

He reached out and took her hand, his smile falsely fond, and again answered, "Not when I can be alone with you, gorgeous."

Beany drew her hand away. You're putting on an act, she thought. There's something phony about this whole deal. She glanced over at the girl in the square-necked yellow dress. There were bands of purple and deeper yellow on the skirt, and she wore a wide lavender belt with it. She had a frail, flowerlike prettiness . . . and she had looked at Beany out of wretched, reproachful eyes.

Ty hitched his chair closer and again hooked his white-coated arm through hers. "Aren't you having fun? You always laugh so much, and here you sit, sober as an owl."

She blinked her shadowed eyes in puzzlement. Was *she* expected to put on an act, too? She tried to make conversation. She nodded toward a nearby table where a couple and two small boys drank coke. "I suppose they're the chaperones."

Ty's eyes flicked in their direction. "Yeh, the Merriweathers. He drove one of the buses in." He added on a belittling laugh, "Old MacLeod, the big-shot principal, always sees that these trips are well chaperoned. Oh my, yes."

"Is Mr. MacLeod here?"

"Not this trip. And, believe it or not, I'm disappointed."

It bothered Beany that she and Ty were at the dance, and yet not part of it. She'd like to be introduced to the Tysonites, to visit with them. She'd even like to explain that she wasn't usually so frou-frou, and that she was in borrowed clothes. She couldn't drink all her Seven-Up. She wanted to hand it across to one of those towheaded little Merriweathers who was asking for another drink, but the parents had lowered their eyes when Beany looked their way.

At the first note from Benny Boden's orchestra, Ty leaped to his feet with a swagger and flourish. "Come on—the night is waning." As though he couldn't wait to dance with her.

As they passed the crowded tables, Beany felt again the condemning coldness of all those eyes. She thought of Dulcie's saying, "Every eye will follow you." She had never thought she would be so chilled by it.

She and Ty were the first ones on the dance floor. He

146

held her so close that her feet stumbled over his; and she thought, with a surge of anger, He's overdoing this devoted cheek-to-cheek stuff.

She wrestled out of his arms, said on a sudden impulse, "Excuse me." She left him and the dance floor and skirted the area of tables toward a door marked Rose Room. For suddenly she could not bear being the only one wearing large and flashy earrings and flaunting an orchid on her wrist. Maybe, if she worked carefully with tissues, she could wipe some of the make-up off her eyes. She was suddenly sick of looking like a *femme fatale*.

In the door of the Rose Room, with its rose carpeting and vanity benches of blond wood, she stopped short. A bevy of Tyson High girls was there. They were gathered around the girl in the yellow dress whom Ty had called Elaine. Elaine was crying.

They saw Beany, then, and stiffened as though an enemy had invaded their camp. Elaine darted one look at her and then fled across the room and through one of the swinging doors that insured privacy for her tears.

Slowly Beany walked over and sat down on one of the benches in front of the wall-length mirror. The Tyson girl who was sitting on the next bench got up and moved away. The group of girls seemed to draw together by a mutual bond of resentment. And she, Beany, was the outsider.

She could only sit there in such acute discomfort that she forgot why she had so hurriedly left Ty in the middle of a dance. The girls were muttering together, but muttering loud enough for her to catch some of the words . . . "Strutting around in a white coat" . . . "He's got a nerve —after losing the championship for us" . . . She even caught the word, "Elaine."

And then Elaine herself scuttled out of her hiding place

and toward the door. The others closed in protectingly behind her, casting a last baleful glance at the girl in front of the mirror as they left.

Slowly and with awkward fingers, Beany unsnapped Dulcie's earrings, wrapped them in tissue and put them in her bag. She untied the ribbon that held the wilting orchid on her wrist. She laid it on the glass top of the long dressing table. Once Andy had sent her an orchid, and she had pressed it between the pages of her scrapbook. But not this one. Her lips twisted in irony. The money for it, as well as for Ty's white coat, should have been added to the Sinking Fund.

Around the numb enclosure of her mind one question kept repeating itself: Why did the Tysonites resent her so? She sat on and on, hating the thought of going back on the dance floor. Shivering again, she got to her feet and left the Rose Room.

It had turned colder. A damp chill in the air pricked at her bare arms. She wished she had brought a wrap.

Ty was not on the dance floor. It was not hard to ascertain that at a glance, because his white coat had stood out among the casually dressed boys. He was not at any of the tables either. There seemed to be a thinning out of the dancers, a scurrying about for sweaters and lunch baskets.

Maybe Ty had had enough and gone out to their car. Well, so had she had enough, thank you. She went down the steps into the grounds. Thunder rumbled in the sky and a zigzag of lightning suddenly showed up the buildings, the trees, the people.

She was walking toward the parking space when she saw Ty. He was slumped down on a long bench under a tree. Beany dropped down beside him. He didn't say anything

148

as he turned expressionless eyes toward her. She said with a bright edge to her voice, "Remember me? I'm the girl you came with—the girl everyone's been glowering at all evening."

"They hate me," he muttered.

"I gathered as much," she said shortly.

She felt suddenly tired and chilled; and her burn, irritated by the tight ribbon band, was throbbing. She said, "There's no use in sitting here and getting wet. It's been an expensive enough evening without my having to send Dulcie's dress to a cleaner."

He didn't answer. He stared moodily ahead of him, his broad shoulders hunched under the white coat.

The wind rose and with it a spate of rain. And through it, like a great flurry of leaves, ran the noisy, laughing Tyson High group with sweaters over their heads. Mr. Merriweather, the chaperone, scooped his smaller son up in his arms. And the two on the bench heard the roar of the bus motors. Tyson High was starting for home after the day at Acacia Gardens Amusement Park.

This time it was Ty who said, as he got to his feet, "No use sitting here. Let's go."

A few raindrops pelted them as they hurried to the car. They had reached the park gates and turned south when the downpour came. Ty asked, as Beany shivered beside him, "Want my coat?" She said, "No, thanks," and went on hugging her goose-pimply arms to her. I don't want anything from you, she thought angrily.

At last, Beany's curiosity was too much for her. "Why didn't you mix with the Tyson crowd? Why did they act the way they did toward you—us?"

He muttered some evasive answer about their being a

bunch of hicks. She pursued, "I heard the girls talking in the dressing room. They said something about *you* losing Tyson the championship. What'd they mean?"

He drove for a full minute with the wipers slashing across the wet windshield before he answered, "I quit school. I left town before our game with Sun Ridge. If we'd won it, Tyson would have had the championship."

Her thoughts flashed back to that flattering write-up. "If Ty pitches his same airtight game two weeks from today—"

"You mean you quit school and left town in a huff? And so you didn't pitch the Sun Ridge game, and they lost the Valley Prep championship? Why did you leave them in the lurch like that?"

She thought he wasn't going to answer. He stopped for a red light that was a blur in the rain. He waited for the green signal and drove on before he rasped out, "Because I'd had all I could take, that's why."

And then the story came out.

All through high school, Ty had gone with Elaine Mac-Leod, who was a year behind him, and the daughter of the high-school principal. Ty had spent about as much time in the MacLeod home as he had in his own.

In late March came the regional Forensic Meet. Elaine had been one of the debaters, and Ty was to drive her and another couple to the little town where the debate was to take place.

"Elaine didn't have a chance to place in it and she knew it," he said. "I didn't see why we should waste a perfectly good Saturday night going to a fool thing like that and sitting around listening to a lot of kids get up and stammer through their speeches. So I talked the other couple and Elaine into stopping off at a barn dance instead."

"Gosh!" Beany said under her breath.

"It would've been all right," he defended. "No one would have known the difference if Elaine hadn't chickened out on the whole thing the next day and admitted to her dad that we didn't show up at the debate. That's what came of her having a teacher for a father. He hit the ceiling. Monday he called all four of us into his office. He raised the roof with us—you'd have thought we committed murder. And as a matter of discipline, said he, he was suspending all of us for two weeks."

"Even Elaine, his own daughter? Well, at least he was fair about it."

"Fair?" he almost yelled at Beany. "That's what Elaine said. But then she would—she was so under her father's thumb. I'll bet if Dad had been alive, he'd have been on my side. Of course, Mom works under MacLeod and she seems to think he's Jehovah. Well, not me. I told him that if he kicked me out of school for two weeks, I'd stay kicked out and he could give my baseball suit to someone else."

"I suppose you thought you could put the heat on, and because you were the winning pitcher, you'd be let off while the others took the rap?"

"Why should anyone take a rap for going to a dance on Saturday night? Why should Elaine buckle under to her father like a scared sheep? That's when we had our fight."

And that's why he had wanted to take a party doll to the Tyson dance night at Acacia and wave her in front of Elaine. He had meant it—only not what Beany thought he meant—when he said, "I've got to take you to Acacia and dance tomorrow night, if it's the last thing I ever do." Sure, he'd had to, complete with white coat, to make all of Tyson think he was a big shot in Denver, just as he had been in Tyson before that matter of discipline came up.

151

And then the whole evening's hurt and disappointment boiled up inside her. "You're more than a spoiled athlete," she flung out. "You're a spoiled brat. A lot you care about making a fool of me—a lot you care about Elaine feeling so hurt—" She stopped there. She wouldn't give him the satisfaction of knowing that Elaine had cried over it. "Well, I hope you're happy with the phony act you put on tonight."

Her anger spent, she subsided. Neither one spoke on the long ride across town. The rain had slacked to a drizzle by the time Ty turned into their driveway. The minute the car stopped, she got out and, bundling her tulle skirts about her, ran for the shelter of the porch. Her only concern was in keeping Dulcie's dress dry.

The house was dark except for the hall light. Johnny must not have come home from the TV station yet. Thank goodness, Lisa was asleep and could ask no questions about Beany's wonderful evening. She didn't want to tell her how *un*-wonderful it had been. And, thank goodness, Miss Rutledge wasn't the kind of chaperone to wait up.

Beany took off her pumps and very quietly climbed the stairs to her room. She heard Ty come in and, as stealthily as she, go to the room he shared with Johnny.

Her teeth were chattering as she took off Dulcie's dress, shook out its skirt, and hung it on a hanger. She didn't want to tell Dulcie, either, about this chilling, somehow shaming, evening.

She still shivered as she pulled on her scanty pajamas and crawled into bed.

Lying there in the dark, she felt an ache of longing for Andy. He was the one person she could tell about it. He always understood. She wished she could say to him in person—or even by letter, "Andy, I've made such a mess of things." But when he came back to Denver now, it would be that Sylvia somebody he'd be getting in touch with. And there was the blonde in the dark glasses at San Diego.

Beany muttered aloud, "Everything started going wrong the night I swiped the flare off the highway." For if she hadn't had the giveaway black pot in her car, she'd have had a happy evening instead of a rift with Andy. If it hadn't been for the rift, if there had been letters going back and forth, it wouldn't have seemed so—so necessary for her to go on a date with Ty.

18

THE next morning dawned chill and gloomy with driz-
zling skies—poor drying weather for that reluctant patch
of paint in the rumpus room.

Beany was getting the vacuum cleaner out of the hall
closet for the Saturday cleaning when Ty came down the
stairs on dragging feet. There was nothing of the cocky
and wisecracking Ty in him this morning. He looked
heavy-eyed and wretched, and Beany's heart melted as he
fumbled out, "I'm sorry about last night, Beany."

She gave him a shaky smile of reconciliation. "That's all
right, Ty. I guess I'll live through it."

"I was a long time going to sleep—and I kept thinking
how low-down it was of me. I mean, I didn't think about
it beforehand, because all I could think about—"

"I know," Beany said. "Funny, what crazy things people
do to show themselves—or somebody else—that they don't
care."

With that Johnny came out of the kitchen, saying, "Ty,
I've just been waiting to ask you—" He broke off as he

looked at their sober faces. "Is this a private fight or can I get in?"

Neither one answered.

Johnny stood leaning against the closet door. He was always tired the morning after the TV show; his face looked thinner, his black wet-feather hair seemed longer. But this morning his eyes were alert with plans.

"What'd you want to ask me?" Ty muttered.

"I want you to do something for me. I brewed up some fresh coffee. Come on out in the kitchen. You both look as though you could stand a bracer."

In the kitchen Johnny explained: Last night's program of bringing the train to Denver had wound up the historic events. The next series was to be on early towns and their founders. "I was telling the prof about Tyson, because I remembered your saying that your forebears stopped off there to summer their cattle—"

"Dad's grandfather planted the first sugar beet in that region," Ty put in with something of pride, as he poured cream in his coffee.

"Yeh, that's the kind of color we want. Do your folks have any early-day pictures or journals?"

Ty gave a grunting laugh. "The town's running over with them. Mom keeps some under lock and key at the school library. And MacLeod, the principal, has gathered up a lot, too, because last summer he put on a festival to celebrate the seventy-fifth birthday of the town."

Johnny said happily, "This will be duck soup. It's always easier if you have someone to introduce you around, instead of tackling it cold. So how about your going out to Tyson with me?"

The cup in Ty's hand dropped with a small bang into he saucer. He looked helplessly at Beany, then at Johnny.

155

He said harshly, "I can't go back to Tyson. I'm in the dog-house out there."

Johnny said on a sober grin, "I sort of figured you might be. But you don't want to stay in the doghouse for keeps, do you?"

"It's too late now," Ty said, his face slack with misery. "Every letter I get from Mom, she keeps wanting me to come back. And maybe I could have, if I hadn't made such a jackass out of myself last night—"

Beany put in, "Ty had a fight with his girl out in Tyson, and that's why he took me to the dance. It was Tyson night at Acacia." She turned to Ty, "But it still isn't too late. I was so mad last night I wouldn't tell you—but Elaine was crying in the Rose Room when I went in."

He looked jolted and repeated in unbelief, "Elaine . . was . . . crying?"

Beany nodded firmly. "I'm just sure she expected you to turn up at the dance as her date."

"For three years Elaine and I always went to the picnic and dance together—but I—well, I thought she didn' care—"

"You could still make it all right with her," Beany insisted.

"But I don't know about her dad and the rest of the town," he muttered. "I wish now I'd never left the way I did. I guess I've always wished it, only I wouldn't admit it."

Johnny said in a casual voice, "This program we did last night was about runners-away, and how they had to face what they ran away from. Sounds corny, but it makes sense."

Ty was turning his coffee cup round and round in its saucer. Beany sensed the battle he was waging with him self. Go back, she was silently urging, go back to Tyson and Elaine.

She poured more coffee and said kindly, "Drink your coffee, Ty. How about some toast?"

He didn't answer her. He looked at Johnny and asked in a strained voice, "When d'you want to go?"

"The sooner, the better. Any chance you could go to-day?"

Ty lifted his eyes to the rain-misted window, said in a voice that was both scared and resolute, "It's never so busy at the creamery on a rainy day. And the boss's wife has been coming in to help lately." The scraping of his chair sounded loud in the kitchen as he pushed it back and stood up. Even though his eyes were focused on some distant and unhappy point, his face was set. "Yeh, the sooner, the better. I'll call the creamery and ask."

"Tell them," Beany prompted, "that you have urgent business in Tyson." Tell them, she wanted to add, that your whole future depends on it.

In less than half an hour the two set out in Johnny's car for Tyson. Beany ran out just as they reached the gate for one final admonition to Ty. "Be sure to tell Elaine that I'm not the orchid-on-the-wrist kind."

He grinned shakily. "O.K., I'll tell her about your fryin' arm."

They didn't come back that night.

Beany watched for them, going to the door now and then to look out. It was a dark, wet night, the kind when not many people would be on the highway going to Twin Pine. If only she had a car, she could take that ill-gotten flare back and drop it any place where she saw the John Starr Company sign. Surely, with that off her shoulders, she wouldn't feel so crossgrained with life.

On Sunday evening Johnny returned—alone. To an impatient Beany and Lisa he explained that Ty's mother had needed his help. An addition had been built to the school library, which meant a great deal of shifting furniture and books. So Ty had called the creamery from Tyson, and his boss told him they could finish out the summer without Ty.

Johnny was rumpled and tired and sunburned, and loaded down with old pictures, newspapers, and letters. "That's a regular gold mine of material out there. Can you imagine it—I met one old-timer, who's touching ninety, who actually came out in the wagon train that stopped there? He was the one who located water for them to put down wells—and with a forked stick he called a doodlebug."

"Never mind the doodlebugger," Beany said. "Tell us more about Ty. Who did he go to see first? What did Mr. MacLeod say—I mean, was he nice?"

"What about Elaine?" Lisa asked.

Johnny dropped his long length on the couch. "Yes, you human question marks, everybody was nice—after the ice was once broken. We got to Tyson and stopped in front of the school, because Ty figured his mother would be there, working in the library. We were going up the steps just as MacLeod was coming out. I never saw a guy so scared as Ty was when he looked up and saw him."

"What'd he say? What'd Ty say?"

Johnny chuckled. "We all just stood there for what you might call a pregnant moment and then Ty mumbled out that he'd come back—that he guessed nobody wanted to see him—"

Beany breathed out, "I can't bear it if MacLeod acted chilly."

"He didn't. He shook hands with him and said, 'I'm glad to see you back, son.' So then we all went in and saw Ty's mother—and she's got pictures of Tyson when the cottonwoods were just little buggywhips—"

"Let's get to Elaine," Beany prompted.

"Elaine?" Johnny asked, as though he didn't know whom they were talking about. "You mean MacLeod's daughter? I wasn't in on that meeting, so you'll have to let your imagination fill in on what he said and what she said. But everything seems to have been neatly patched up, because Ty's going to school at Tyson next year."

"You mean he isn't going to the U?"

"He wouldn't have enough credits to get in there this fall. He's been a washout at summer school. He and Elaine evidently worked out a cozy arrangement. He'll take the classes he needs to get his high school diploma and then they'll start to college together. Elaine will drive Ty in at the end of next week to get his luggage."

"He still owes Beany some board," Lisa said.

Johnny answered on a prodigious yawn, "He'll pay it. He's on MacLeod's payroll as book-mover. In fact, if Elaine's dad had asked him to clean sewers, I think he'd have leaped at the chance. Any more questions?"

"No, I guess not," Beany said. "Except, are you hungry?"

Wonder of wonders, Johnny shook his head. "I'm bulging from the fatted calves that were killed for the prodigal's return—only the calves were frying chickens. And sweet corn, and apple pie. . . ."

Johnny fell asleep on the couch. Beany moved restlessly through the house. Johnny had dropped his car keys on the coffee table beside the couch. Lisa sat close to the TV

159

set with the sound turned low, absorbed in a mystery. Miss Rutledge was reading or studying in her room.

Why couldn't Beany take back the black pot tonight? She would rather someone went with her, so that when she slowed the car on a stretch of road under construction by the John Starr Company, that someone could gently drop out the flare.

She looked at Lisa. She wished now she had told her the truth that first evening, instead of skirting around it, when Lisa was so concerned over Beany's returning without Andy. For it would be hard now to say, "Lisa, I lied to you. I stole a highway flare. Come and help me take it back."

No, Beany would have to manage it alone.

She picked up Johnny's car keys, muttering to the absorbed Lisa that she was going on an errand. She took the want-ad section of the Sunday paper and made her way to the basement furnace room. The round black pot looked uglier and greasier than ever as she swaddled it in newspaper. There was still oil in it.

Warily she came up the steps and softly pushed open the screen of the side door. She had to push the curious dog aside with her foot as she went out. She had no sooner gone down the two steps when Red gave an announcing bark and, almost simultaneously, the front doorbell pealed loudly.

Now who could that be? But whoever it was, the ringing would rouse Johnny, who could wake up as readily as he could drop off to sleep. She stood there, clutching her burden, not knowing whether to make a run for the basement or for the car.

Neither—for Johnny was in the hall, calling, "Beany, where are you? Get a vase—or maybe two."

The only thing she could do was to chuck the pot hurriedly under the steps. She was just straightening up when Johnny came to the door, bearing an armful of gladioli. Lisa was behind him. "Oh, there you are, Beany," he said.

Beany came into the hall, the car keys jingling on her finger. "I just thought I'd—oh, take a little ride up to the Robin—and tell Dulcie about Ty—"

"All right, let's," he said. "Only I'd better go with you, because the brake is sticking worse than ever. Here, do something with these." He thrust the flowers into her arms.

"Who brought them?" she asked.

"Judge Buell. He just stopped to leave them for us."

Wouldn't you know! If there were any plans of Beany's to be upset, it would be Judge Buell who would upset them.

And so on another night Beany waited for the house to quiet down. Again she got up and stealthily descended the stairs in her bare feet. She had already thought out another hiding place for the highway flare.

This time she took it out from under the steps and carried it up to the room over the garage, where for years the Malones had stored castoff furniture, skis, and sleds, as well as old radios and lamps which they hoped some day to repair.

Beany's eyes didn't linger on any of that, but sought instead a dress form that stood unsteadily on its iron frame, encased in a discarded blanket robe. Headless Hetty, the Malones called it, and someone had even stuck a vase in the hollow neck and set a hat rakishly on top of it.

It was under Headless Hetty's dusty bathrobe, and where her feet would be if she had feet instead of stopping at the hips, that Beany wedged the wrapped flare and draped the bottom of the old robe over it.

19

JENNIFER REED telephoned Beany the next morning.

"At long last, Beany, all the remodeling and redecorating are done. Just be thankful that you don't have realtor-minded parents who think a house has to be a showplace. So I'm lining up the staff party to welcome in Beany, the new editor. I'm calling you first to know if you are free this coming Saturday night."

Hah, as though every Saturday night weren't free for Beany Malone. "Free as the wind," she answered.

Jennifer said, with an apologetic laugh, "I'm just barely getting my party out of the way in time for you to hold the first staff meeting at your house."

Oh dear, and Beany had been so sure that her first meeting would be held in a rumpus room with red carpeting on which sat many tub chairs with bright cushions. She said wistfully, "How do the bullfighting scenes on your rumpus room walls look?"

"Quite colorful and splashy with red capes, bullfighter, and bull. So I thought I'd have a South-of-the-Border theme for the party. Maybe you've got a bright-colored, swishy skirt—"

"I have! Adair sent me one, and it's fairly crying to be swished. Is it a date party, Jennifer? I mean, are the ones on the staff to bring their Old Faithfuls or near Old Faithfuls, as Dulcie calls them?" She was thinking of Rosellen and her hope of going to Jennifer's party on Sidney's "coat tails."

There was a small pause at Jennifer's end. "No, Beany, just the staff and our sponsor, Mrs. Brierly. Because—well, the rumpus room isn't too large—"

Beany thought of that spacious pink house, the covered patio, the lily pool, and the great sloping lawns. But, sensing some embarrassment at Jennifer's end, she hastened to say, "Yes, I know. If all the staff turns out, it makes a gang of twenty or so."

"That's right," Jennifer agreed, and ended, "I'll call all the others right away."

Beany replaced the telephone and stood there only a brief moment while her jaw set stubbornly. The second coat of red paint *had* to go on her basement floor this morning.

The whirr of the lawnmower came through the open doors. She walked to a window and looked out. Johnny was cutting their lawn, and Lisa was trimming the tall grass around shrubs and flower beds. That was fine. Beany wouldn't ask Lisa to help, because she would be sure to say, "But, Beany, you can't put another coat of paint over paint that isn't dry yet."

Wet or dry, the second coat was going on.

163

She went down to the basement and pried the lid off the bucket of red paint, her eyes reading again, "Paint the floor in the morning. Walk on it in the evening."

She dipped her brush in the paint and stroked over the wet spot. An unexpected thing happened. The paint already on the floor came off on the brush. No matter how she tried, she couldn't get the paint to cover. This nondrying paint reminded her of fudge. If it was runny and sticky when you poured it onto a plate, you could let it sit till doomsday, and it would never harden. But, at least, you could recook fudge.

That accursed diesel oil from that accursed black pot. Beany, with streaks of cherry red paint on her knees, even on the soles of her feet (for she had taken off her loafers for the job) finally put the cover back on the paint bucket in frustrated fury.

And because it is always easier to be furious at someone else, instead of one's self, her anger reached out for someone to fasten on. Judge Buell! It was all his fault. If it hadn't been for him and his sending Miss Rutledge, she could have boarded two young men. And if she had, she could have afforded carpet for this room—wall-to-wall carpeting that would have covered the floor, oil seepage or no.

She dropped down on a backless chair in the laundry part of the basement and sat there, a box of soap powder pressing into her back, muttering over and over, "Him, and his talk about a sobering influence."

She heard the slam of the side door, an extra commotion and laughter. Mary Fred must have bobbed in again. Sure enough, she called down the basement steps, "Beany, if you're down in the dungeon, come on up," and leaned over the stair rail as Beany climbed the steps to ask, "What're you doing—painting?"

"If you must know," Beany answered wryly, "I was just sitting down there hating Judge Buell."

Mary Fred's rippling laugh rang out. "Don't talk like that. Who knows? With that bashful Carlton always running to you for cover, you might be talking about your future father-in-law."

"Heaven forbid!" Beany said sourly.

Mary Fred looked dressed-up and pretty in her lavender sunback dress. Lisa and Miss Rutledge came to welcome her. Johnny hurried in the back door from his lawn cutting. "Ah, the meeter and greeter again," he said.

"Nuh-uh, this trip is different. I brought Mr. Billings, an oil-man guest, down from the ranch for an important business conference. And look!" She took out of her purse a small white card and held it up. "In appreciation, he gave me his card at the Capitol Club and told me to take all my family and friends to lunch there while he was at his meeting. Just give the waiter his number, said he, and go whole hog. He said he'd be hurt if we didn't. So all of you scrub behind your ears and come along. You, too, Lisa. And you, Miss Rutledge."

Miss Rutledge thanked her for the invitation, but said she had some books she must take back to the library.

"That's all right," Mary Fred overrode her. "I'll drop you off at the library afterwards. It isn't every day you get to slurp up vichyssoise, courtesy of a Texas oil man."

Lisa was more firm. "Mary Fred, I'd like to, but I—well, I'd just eat too much, and besides I want to be here when the mail comes. You see, Joe said they were going to fire the range Friday, and he was to let me know how he qualified—and I just can't wait—"

Mary Fred patted her. "I understand, honey. Time was
—in my dim and distant past—when a letter meant that
much to me. Hurry along and depaint yourself, Beany.
And you get yourself into a tie, Johnny. They won't let
you in the Capitol Club—to which only men of capital
belong—without one."

"A tie it is. I always wanted to order Rock Cornish Hen
and see what was rocky or corny about it."

Beany's low spirits welcomed this respite. It would be
wonderful to get away from the house—and from herself.
She laughed in reckless exuberance. "I'll depaint myself,
and lipstick myself, and you wear your hat with the flowers
on it, Miss Rutledge."

Miss Rutledge not only wore her hat with the flowers
on it, but a frilly blouse with the chalk-dust suit.

The four were in high spirits as they drove downtown
in the ranchwagon and into the parking lot that served
patrons of the Capitol Club.

They rode up in the elevator to the top floor of the
building and stepped into the foyer with its thick green
carpet dusted with gold. Just as Beany was looking at the
immense curved divans in block print and thinking, A
family of six could sleep on one, Johnny was saying, "I
knew a fellow whose father once owned the ground this
club is built on, and he traded it for a team of horses."

A man turned away from a group of men to greet them.
It was Judge Buell. He shook hands all around, and listened while Mary Fred explained that this celebration was
because of her driving one of the members down from the
Lazy J and back again.

He chuckled as Johnny said, "You might know it's an
occasion when I'm behind a tie."

166

The judge beamed benignly on Beany and Miss Rutledge. "I'm so glad our little arrangement worked out so —er—happily for everyone."

"It's been very happy for me," Miss Rutledge said. Beany didn't know what to say.

There was no wall between the foyer and dining room, but only a low partition of black glass with a gold design on it. Judge Buell walked with them to the entrance to the dining room. An affable man with a rose in his buttonhole and a large writing pad stood guard there. He bowed to them, glanced at the card Mary Fred extended, and asked, "And under what name is the reservation?" He bent his head to scan his list.

Mary Fred looked dashed. "Reservation? Oh, I didn't know . . . You see, I drove Mr. Billings down from the Lazy J and he told me—"

"I'm sorry, Miss, but every table is full except the ones that have been reserved."

"How long would we have to wait?" Johnny asked.

"I couldn't say—exactly." The keeper of the door glanced back at one end of the foyer where groups of people sat, some with drinks on the tables before them, some visiting. "There are quite a few ahead of you." He added with gentle reproof, "We have to honor the reservations, you see."

He looked up then and saw Judge Buell, and with a murmured, "Nice to see you, Judge," stepped aside with deference. The judge, with the firm tread of one sure of being seated, went in.

Wouldn't you know, Beany thought, he would be in and we would be out! The sheep and the goats.

They turned back from the dining room, feeling

167

strangely rebuffed and letdown. Mary Fred murmured, "We'd have to wait a long time—and I have to pick up Mr. Billings at three." It was now one thirty.

Johnny suggested halfheartedly, "We can always go to the Keg down in the next block and have us a hot-dog."

"Oh, no!" Mary Fred wailed. "Not with all us females in white gloves and heels. And me in earrings."

They were still standing, irresolute and forlorn, when a waiter hurried up to them and asked, "Are you the Malone party of four? Come with me, I have a table for you."

They followed him to a table in the corner with a view of both the gold-domed capitol and the mountains in the distance. One waiter pulled out chairs, covered in white leather, and seated them at a table with a beige damask cloth and a low centerpiece of pink roses, surrounded by a multitude of small, white candles. Another tendered them menus and whisked a "Reserved" sign off the table.

Johnny grinned up at the waiter. "Lucky for us, somebody with a reservation didn't show up."

"This is Judge Buell's table, sir. We always hold it for him on Mondays. But he told the headwaiter he wanted you to have it today."

"How nice of him," Mary Fred exclaimed. "Where is he? We'd like to thank him."

"He went out through the Men's Bar, Miss. All he said was to see that you young folks got his table."

They looked at each other. So Judge Buell had saved their day for them and, not even wanting thanks, had quietly eased out. Mary Fred sent a reproachful glance to Beany. "Now aren't you ashamed of being so busy hating our next-door neighbor?"

Beany nodded sheepishly. "I'll really feel kind of lost

without having him to blame things on," she admitted.

"You get lopsided if you carry a grudge too long," Johnny said.

The fun of ordering from the immense menus, and of Johnny's saying, "It's these decisions that are so wearing," and finally ordering steak on a flaming sword instead of Rock Cornish Hen. The waiter recommended chicken salad in a pineapple boat for the ladies, and the ladies ordered it. Beany basked in it all; the frequent passing of hot popovers and raspberry jam, the Yes ma'ams and the No ma'ams.

At last they sat back, replete and relaxed, with only their iced coffee to toy with. How flushed and happy Miss Rutledge looked—and how much she seemed to be one of them.

Johnny and Mary Fred looked over the large room to see if they knew anyone. Johnny did. He said, "There's the photographer from the TV station. Hey, Mary Fred, he's talking of going up to the Lazy J for a weekend. He was asking me about rates. Why don't we go over and talk to him?"

When Johnny and Mary Fred had left the table, Miss Rutledge reached out and touched Beany's hand. "I don't blame you a bit, child, for resenting Judge Buell's pushing me off onto you. I must have seemed terribly stiff and unfriendly."

Beany said honestly, "I was in a bad mood that night you came. I shouldn't have acted so crummy."

"I have something to confess, too. I've never felt at home with young people. I've always been afraid of them. It seems to me that I was never young—that I went from fifteen to being an old maid schoolteacher."

"Mary Fred said your father was sick for a long time. Was that what you meant when you said—you know, about being afraid to go places?"

"Yes. I was a sophomore in high school when our old touring car turned over with my parents and injured them badly. Mother died within a few months, but Father lived on—a sick and unhappy and demanding man." She hesitated, then added, "He was sick mentally, as well, because he blamed himself for the accident."

She went on in the flat voice of unhappy remembering. It had been almost impossible to get anyone to care for him, so all through high school, all through her college days, she had hurried to classes, hurried home. There had been no going out, no company in that melancholy house.

"And did you start teaching when you were through college?" Beany asked.

"I had to, because we needed the money. It was just changing one set of schoolroom walls for others. My father's sister looked after him through the day. He died seven years ago, when I was almost forty."

She took a sip of iced coffee, smiled quaveringly. "But what I started to tell you was that I'll never feel such a big gap between me and young folks like you again. You see, the school principal has been wanting me to teach literature in the high school, but I've always been afraid to make the change. I felt so much safer with my eight- and nine-year-olds. I never realized that you young folks had your own problems and heartaches and insecurities."

"Funny, isn't it?" Beany said. "It's so easy for us to think grownups haven't a care in the world."

Miss Rutledge chuckled, "And so easy for us to think you teen-agers haven't."

Mary Fred and Johnny came back to the table. She said,

170

"Our slumming party is over. I'll drop all you folks off and just have time to pick up our absent, but genial, host."

She let Miss Rutledge and Johnny off at the campus library and turned toward Barberry Street. As she slowed in front of the house, Beany said with a sigh, "I hate to come home—and back to my losing battle with the rumpus room."

"Oh, Beaver, does getting that rumpus room still mean so much to you?"

"Yes, it does. I pictured it as such a bright and pretty—"

"Haven and retreat," Mary Fred murmured. "I still don't see why you want one, but I'm sorry things have gone so wrong. Why won't the paint dry?"

"It's not only the paint," Beany evaded. "It's just that everything has gone so wrong."

Mary Fred glanced at Beany's wristwatch. "I wish I had more time to pry into what and why everything has gone wrong for you. But I can't keep Mr. Billings waiting. You don't have to let them go on being wrong, do you? Why don't you do something about it?"

"I don't know what to do," Beany muttered as she got out of the car.

Lisa was sitting on the porch steps waiting for her. She was wrapped in starry-eyed happiness, and Beany said, "So you got your letter?"

"More than a letter. Look." Lisa took the lid off a small velvet-lined box and held it out to show Beany, who stared stupidly at a silver bar to which was attached a medal in the shape of a square cross.

"What is it?" she asked.

"It's a sharpshooting medal," Lisa said, her eyes shining. "Joe sent it to me. He won it and he wanted me to have it."

Maybe Andy Kern had won one, too. Beany wondered which girl he had given his to.

"I'm going to wear it all the time," Lisa said. "It's the first present I ever got from a boy. And I have something else to tell you, Beany. I'm so happy—and you know you just can't hate people when you're happy. And all at once I didn't feel mean toward Mom and Jeanie—I never did feel that way about Dad. I even saw their side of it. Now that I've lost almost twenty pounds, I know myself what an eyesore I was to them. What I mean is, it just came over me how hateful and stubborn I'd been all summer—and so I wrote to the folks."

"You did!"

"Yes, and I told Jeanie I didn't blame her for not wanting me for a bridesmaid."

"She isn't going to be married until fall. I'll bet anything she will want you now."

Lisa said softly, "Maybe she will. But it doesn't seem so important now—really, it doesn't. I don't expect to hear from the folks right away, because they usually go to the cottage on the lake the middle of August. But anyway, I feel better about it all—and sort of peaceful and happy inside."

Beany leaned against the warm porch pillar. What a coincidence it was that, even while Johnny was writing about early-day runners-away, two present-day ones, Lisa and Ty, should find shelter at the Malones'. Strange, too, that Beany had been the one to urge Ty to make things right, and he had; she had helped Lisa to smooth out her life. Yet Beany's own was still anything but smooth. She was not peaceful and happy inside.

Lisa was saying, "Maybe it was the letter from Joe that decided me. Because he sounds so nice and so good. And

172

his folks aren't the kind to fight. They even drove from Kansas clear out to San Diego to visit him. Oh, and here are some pictures he sent of the family and some of the fellows. He said Andy was so nice to them—that, on his day off, Andy took them to Coronado."

She stood close to Beany and held out the pictures. "Here're Joe's mother and father and his sister. Which one is Andy?"

"This one is Andy," Beany said in a small voice, indicating him, standing with a middle-aged couple and a girl in dark glasses, and a sweater with a border of flowers down the front. It was the same girl Andy had been leaning on the deck rail with. So it was Kansas's sister, taken when he had been showing the folks around.

Beany, the conclusion-jumper. . . .

She said suddenly, "Lisa, I'm going to write to Andy. Right now."

She went to her room, and pushed aside all the dime-store lotions and perfumes on her dressing table, and wrote swiftly:

> Dear Andy:
> I wanted to go dancing with you that night, but the reason I couldn't was because I stole a highway flare, and if I'd opened the door it would have rolled out, and I didn't want your dad to see it—

She wrote on and on and, as she wrote, gentle tears rolled down her cheeks without her heeding them. Like Lisa, she felt a vast contentment and relief.

> If I ever get a chance I'll take the fool pot back where I got it, but you know how hard it is around here to do anything on the q.t.

20

DULCIE LUNGAARDE came in the next afternoon and said without preamble, "I got the good word from Jennifer that her party is coming off Saturday night and that it's to be a South-of-the-Border affair, so let's have a look at those tiered skirts you two have, because I'm going to make one for myself."

She broke off to say, "What's the idea of Jennifer's just having the staff, and no dates? Just enough, said she, to fit into the rumpus room. She's got the whole house, the whole yard. What're those Reeds afraid of—that we'll draw pictures on the wallpaper, or steal a goldfish out of their pool?"

Even though Beany had wondered the same thing, she didn't like Dulcie's criticism of Jennifer, her idol. She diverted her by asking, "So you're going to make yourself a fiesta skirt?"

"*And* a sheer blouse for me, and the one I promised Lisa

and you should have one, too. Penney's are having a sale on figured prints and white goods. It only takes a scrap for a blouse. Lisa, does your skirt fasten yet?"

Lisa raced up the stairs and soon reappeared in the purple skirt which she held together at the waistband. "It'll zip up now, but it won't button," she said.

"We're practically there," Dulcie praised, noting that the buttonhole could almost touch the edge of the button. "A couple more days—why, by the time I get your blouse whipped up, you'll be ready for the picture to send Joe Kansas."

"His name is Kaswell," Lisa corrected her. "I don't think the fellows ought to call him Kansas."

Dulcie planned on. "I'll bring my portable machine over here, because Dad's doing some wiring in our house and you never know when the juice is going to be turned off." She sat down at the table and riffled through the pages of the morning paper to Penney's ad. "I'd like to get a sort of tawny-looking print to set off my fiery beauty." She turned Lisa's skirt this way and that, gauging the yardage in it. "Six yards," Dulcie announced. "And a breeze to make. All machine work except the gathers."

They were still discussing skirts and low-necked blouses when Beany heard the unmistakable click that meant the mailman had put mail in their box. She went out after it.

More mail from those away from home. A card from Miggs Carmody who, with her parents, was turning homeward. Miggs added to that bit of information, "I can hardly wait to see or hear your surprise." Cards from Beany's father and Adair. "We're homesick. We're starting to pack for the trek home. There'll be a few stopovers. We can hardly wait to be surprised."

Beany had been so sure that she could lead each one of them down the basement steps, throw open the door to the wine room, and ask proudly, "How do you like it?"

And now her surprise would be that there was no surprise. Unless you could call that fiasco of a room with its scabby portion of floor, the one red throw rug, the one tub chair a surprise.

She stood on in the hot sun, wondering when her letter would reach Andy, wondering if he would answer it right away. He *would* answer, wouldn't he, even though she had been so long in writing?

She walked into the house to find Lisa and Dulcie gathered close to Johnny and the telephone in the hallway. Johnny said, "We have news for you, little Beaver."

"News?"

"We're going to have a whale of a party *here* Saturday night."

"Saturday night? Here? But that's the night I'm going to Jennifer's party."

"Jennifer just now called. She said that something had come up so that she couldn't have the party at her house. So I told her just to reroute the whole caboodle to the Malones'. I told her to tell them to bring their dates and we'd dance on the green—meaning the cement apron in front of the garage—and that if she had any L.P.'s to bring them along. Carlton Buell's got a lot of good dance records we can borrow even if he isn't home. By the way, Beany, you're invited."

She said, "But, Johnny, it isn't right for us to have the party here. It's tradition for the outgoing editor to entertain for the incoming editor."

"Tradition, my eye! You make 'em, and you break 'em.

We're making one. Because this will be sort of a Beany-Jennifer party. She said she had already ordered tortillas, and already had a lot of red-checked tablecloths and napkins, and I told her to bring them along. I said I'd brew up a huge pot of chili con carne. And none of this stuff about its being a staff party which would leave me out. Because, precious, I'm a staff member emeritus of old *Hark Ye*. And Lisa here will be the stirrer of the chili."

"And Sidney, the Brain, can bring Rosellen," Dulcie said, "and I'll ask Norbett—I think we'll be on speaking terms by then."

Beany could only stand there, staring at each one. She was always slower than the rest when it came to a sudden shift of plans.

"I wonder why Jennifer couldn't have it at her house," she said. "Is somebody sick?"

Johnny shook his head. "No. I asked her. She sounded kind of unhappy—said she'd explain later."

Dulcie said, "I'll bet her folks didn't want a bunch of young hoodlums coming in and spoiling that picture house of theirs. But the rerouting is swell with me. It'll be swell with everyone. It'll be more fun here at the Malones'. Johnny and I've decided to carry on with the Mexican motif—"

"Tell Beany about the lanterns we're going to make," Lisa prompted.

"Luminarias. For our lighting effect. They have them all over the place in Santa Fe at fiesta time. You take a medium-sized paper sack and fold the top back a quarter of the way, and put about three inches of sand in the bottom. The sand is to keep the sack from blowing over—and also to stick a short candle in. They look like old-fashioned square lanterns when they're lighted. We'll line the driveway with them and put them on top of the arbor. Haven't we got a lot of brown paper sacks and some old candles we can cut down to size?"

Lisa said, "We've got a lot of sacks on the back porch"; and Beany murmured, "There're candles galore in the sideboard drawer."

They were shuffling through the sacks when the doorbell rang. Dulcie answered it. She came back, holding a yellow rectangle, and calling out like a bellboy, "Telegram for Lisa Hold. Miss Hold, please."

Lisa's eyes widened. "For me? I never got a telegram before."

"The idea is to read it," Dulcie said, "before you preserve it in alcohol."

Johnny took it and ripped it open for her. He looked up, his brown eyes dancing. "Lisa, don't be scared—it's good news. You won't have to get your picture taken to send your ardent Marine. He'll see you in the flesh. He's coming."

Still Lisa stood wordless, her lips parted. Beany asked, "When?"

Johnny read the telegram:

GETTING LEAVE. AM FLYING TO DENVER.
HOPE TO SEE YOU SATURDAY EVENING.

"H'm, he could have left out *am* and *to* and *hope* and sent it cheaper. But I suppose money's no object to Romeo."

Lisa could only breathe out, "He's coming! Oh mercy, I wish—I wish I'd lost more pounds."

"What're we waiting for?" Dulcie wanted to know. "A party's coming up. Lisa's boy friend is coming. Let's dash

178

down to Penney's and load up on yard goods so we'll be decked out for the occasion. Come on, Beany—come on, Lisa, we'll go down in our pickup."

Beany reached for the oatmeal box and the Sinking Fund. Lisa pushed close to whisper, "Beany, I'm broke, and I don't know when I'll hear from the folks. I don't want you spending money for a blouse for me. Not when you've had such a hard time saving for your rumpus room."

"First things, first," Beany answered. "Romance first, rumpus room second, right now."

There was still another phone call. This time it was Rosellen Kern, and she said to Beany, "Sidney just called and he said Jennifer just called and *she* said the staff party was to be at the Malones' and dates were allowed. True or false?"

"True," Beany said and heard the glad shriek that the word "party" always elicited from Rosellen. "It sounds like a fine, large evening ahead. Lisa got a telegram from Joe Kansas, and he's getting leave and will be here Saturday. You know Andy's friend Kansas?"

"I know. Wouldn't it be perfect if Andy could come with him?"

"Ye-es," Beany agreed. But she would settle for a letter from him that meant they were back on the old footing.

She could hear the motor running in Dulcie's pickup and hurried to say, "Dulcie and Lisa and I are going down to Penney's to buy print for Dulcie's skirt and white goods for blouses for all of us. How about you? Do you want to swish about in a fiesta skirt?"

Maybe she shouldn't have asked that of a girl on crutches.

But Rosellen answered instantly, "I sure do. Hold on a

179

minute." Beany could hear an earnest argument at Rosellen's end, and then she turned back to say, "We've got some turkey-red calico I can make a skirt out of. Mom bought it for curtains for our sleeping porch, only Dad said it was so red it'd look as if the place was on fire. But it isn't too red for me. Could you buy the goods for my blouse? When and where are you going to do all the sewing?"

"Here. In the morning, because Dulcie has to go to work this afternoon."

"O.K., I'll be there."

Dulcie was honking the horn, calling, "Get a move on, Beany. I have to be at the Robin at four, and you know how long it takes to park and unpark."

Beany, clutching the ten-dollar bill she had grabbed out of the oatmeal box, climbed into the lumpy seat of the pickup beside the two girls. Dulcie swung out of the driveway.

They made their way through the crowded store to the booth where the bright-colored prints were on sale. From there they went to the white goods counter. They bought braid and rickrack and lace and embroidery for trim.

Loaded down with packages, they started out the side door on the main floor. Their way led through the shoe department. A sale was going on there, too. The three halted before a table with gay summer footwear.

Of one accord Beany and Dulcie reached for a pair of gold sandals with purple heels. They seemed made to go with Lisa's purple skirt with its trimming of gold braid. They looked at each other with the same thought: Lisa must never wear her stodgy oxfords, which were all she had, with her new skirt and blouse. They looked at the price tag; and each one held out her palm, containing the money they had left, and tacitly computed that there was just enough between them to buy the sandals for Lisa.

"Look, Lisa," Beany said.

Lisa's eyes lighted. "Oh, lovely! But nosir, Beany, you and Dulcie aren't going to—"

"Try them on," Dulcie ordered.

The slippers fitted Lisa to a T.

Beany walked out of Penney's with four pennies left out of the bill she had started with. But, after all, she had started this romance between a girl who never had a letter from a boy and a boy who never had a letter from a girl.

On the drive home, Lisa clutched the shoe box tightly to her. "I'm just so worried for fear he won't like me."

"Listen to her," Dulcie snorted. "Worried for fear *he* won't like *her*. When I have a blind date, all I worry about is whether I'll like *him* or not."

"But you're you," Lisa said simply, "and I'm me."

And I'm not worried about a date, Beany thought, and will he or won't he like me. I'm just worried about will Andy write or won't he. She asked, "Lisa, how long does it take airmail letters to get back and forth to San Diego?"

The answer came in the voice of authority. "Sometimes just a day each way—but sometimes longer."

If Andy wrote right away, she might hear Wednesday —tomorrow. Surely she would hear by Thursday.

21

THE sewing bee got under way at the Malones' the next morning, which was Wednesday. Five minutes after Dulcie drove up in her father's pickup and carried in the portable sewing machine and set it on the dining table, the room became a noisy and cluttered dressmaking shop. Lengths of bright colored print and small mounds of sheer white goods were piled on table, chairs, and sideboard. Streamers of braid or rickrack or lace tripped the unwary. Spools of thread rolled underfoot.

Rosellen Kern arrived. She came in a bright yellow truck with the sign on it, Johnson Plumbing and Heating.

"Leo happened to stop in next door to fix a faucet," Rosellen explained as a heavyset workman helped her up the steps and carried her bulky package for her, "so I asked him if he'd mind dropping me off when he went back to the shop."

"I was glad to, Rosellen," he said.

And he *was* glad to, Beany realized. His day was given a lift by bringing the friendly Rosellen over in his truck.

In the dining room, Rosellen shook out lengths of the brightest red imaginable, and Dulcie staggered backward and shrieked, "Fire! Fire!"

Rosellen laughed, quite unabashed. "And this, too," she said, dangling lengths of white ball fringe. "As long as I'm using the curtain material, I thought I'd use the trim Mom was going to put on the curtains."

"We saw fiesta skirts with ball fringe," Beany told her.

Dulcie, tape measure around her neck and scissors in hand, gave orders. She measured waistlines. She threaded the machine with orange, red, or white thread. "Just three days to make two tiered skirts and four fiesta blouses," she said. "So it's full steam ahead, my hearties."

Beany would have been more help if she hadn't got up again and again to go to the front door and look out at the mailbox on the gatepost to see if the mailman had come. He came at last—but there was no letter from San Diego. Oh, but she hadn't *really* expected it so soon. Sometimes a day each way, Lisa had said—sometimes longer.

You would have thought it was Johnny's party. He was the one who scurried about, going after sand in Dulcie's pickup for the dozens of luminarias that would light up the grounds. He telephoned here and there about L.P. records for them to dance to. "I've got to locate some extension cords to run from the back porch light to the record player outside," he said.

"What about chairs?" Beany asked. "We won't have enough outdoor ones for everyone when we serve the chili."

"You can rent them from a funeral parlor," Dulcie suggested.

"We're renting nothing we can borrow," Johnny said. "I know! Father Hugh's got chairs up there in his recreation hall—the folding variety. I'll phone and ask about them."

You would have thought it was Dulcie's party, too. They would need a larger table for the serving of their many guests. Dulcie said, "Johnny, Dad's got sawhorses and some wide planks. We can rig up a big long table."

"Sure," Johnny said. "And the ones that don't get to the table fast enough can sit on the steps or the ground."

And you would have thought that Dulcie, not Beany, was the instigator of the romance between Lisa and the Marine she had never seen. As they sewed Dulcie gave her advice, for Lisa alternately trod peaks of rapture and depths of dread.

"Maybe he won't like me," she would worry. "Maybe he'll take one look at me and then catch the next bus back to Kansas."

"Like you, my foot!" Dulcie would snort. "Don't you dare let on to him that you're afraid he won't like you. Don't go spilling out that he's your first date, or that your heart is going pitty-pat. Play it cool. I don't mean to give him the icy treatment—"

Rosellen broke in with a giggle, "Sounds like the directions on the mayonnaise jar: 'Keep cool, but do not freeze.'"

"And another thing!" Dulcie looked up from her stitching to shake an emphatic finger at Lisa. "Don't go telling him why you didn't send him a picture right off. Don't say"—and here Dulcie took on a mimicking voice—"'I

184

had to wait till I reduced because I didn't want you to know I was fat.' Nosir. You just be very airy about it. Tell him every time you had a picture to send him, some other boy friend took it away from you."

And through it all, Lisa would look beseechingly at Beany, and Beany would say, "Just don't worry, Lisa. You'll look so pretty. I'll give you a home permanent."

"How do you think I'd look with a pony tail like Dulcie's? My hair's grown so long."

"I'll fix your hair," Dulcie promised.

No letter came for Beany on Thursday. She came back from pulling the mail out of the box and sorting through it and picked up her white blouse that she had so hastily tossed down. She mistook the back of it for the front and put an extra row of lace on it.

Rosellen quoted her Irish grandmother, "Sure, it'll never show on a galloping horse."

Dulcie had been a little optimistic when she said those tiered skirts were a breeze to make. Besides, Dulcie had to leave early each afternoon for the Ragged Robin. So on Thursday, when Miss Rutledge came in and said, "I've turned in my last term paper at the university—and I'm pretty good at putting in zippers," they greeted her with a joyous whoop.

She worked along with them the rest of the day, sewing. She helped them get dinner and, because the dining table was taken over, ate with them in the kitchen. It was she who helped Johnny figure out the recipe for chili. If one and one-half cups of chili beans, one pound of hamburger, one can of tomatoes made enough for six, how many times should they multiply it for the party?

On Friday morning, Beany gave Lisa her home permanent. She had done most of it upstairs, but she was putting Lisa's soft wet hair up in curls in front of the big dining-room mirror. Beany carried the comb and bobby pins with her when she answered the front door.

It was Jennifer Reed, bringing her donations for the party. Instead of jostling a lot of packages, she carried them in a hamper. She looked as poised, as just right as always. Her white sunback dress showed off her smooth tan, the color of coffee with cream in it.

Jennifer Reed, the girl Beany looked up to and longed to imitate, whose rumpus room had filled her with such envy that she had dedicated her summer to having one as near like it as she could.

"Come in, Jennifer," she said, trying not to act flustered as she ushered her in.

For when had the Malone living room looked worse? On the window seat, on the couch, on the floor sat all those innumerable sacks filled with sand. A chagrined Beany explained, "We had these out on the porch, but when the shower came up last evening we moved them in, because if the sacks get wet they split and spill out sand."

Some sand must have spilled out anyway, for the floors and the rug were gritty underfoot. You'd never find sand in the Reed house.

The dining-room-dressmaking shop was no improvement either. Dulcie stopped the sewing machine to say, "Hello there, Jennifer. We're working like crazy to have our skirts and blouses ready for tomorrow night." And Rosellen appeared in the doorway from the kitchen to explain, "Hello, Jennifer, these are onion tears I'm shedding. Seven times one onion makes a lot of onions."

"We had to seven-times the chili recipe," Beany said, trying to clear enough space on the cluttered dining table for Jennifer to set down her basket. The one room Jennifer must *not* see was the kitchen.

"I brought the tortillas and red-checked tablecloths." Jennifer lifted out a huge and heavy package and handed it to Beany. "And this is the ground round for Johnny's chili."

Ground round! Heretofore, Malone chili had been made with hamburger.

"How many guests do you expect, Beany?" Jennifer asked.

Beany laughed. "It started out with about forty—everyone on the staff and dates. Even Mrs. Brierly called up and said she'd like to bring her husband. Miss Rutledge's summer school is over, but we wouldn't hear of her leaving before the party. Then Lisa and her date."

Dulcie broke in, "This day should go down in history. At last, the buttonhole on Lisa's skirt embraces the button." And Lisa, part of her hair in curlers, part hanging stringy and wet, turned her candid smile on Jennifer to add, "Without my holding my breath."

Johnny came in then, picking his way through the luminarias in the living room. He was carrying a light fixture, and several extension cords, looped over his arm like a lariat.

He greeted the caller, "Jennifer, we've got it made! I've finally rounded up enough cords to hook up the record player. And while I'm about it, I'll rig up a light over the back steps. Beany, where's our brace and bit? I'll have to bore a hole through the porch wall to run the cord through."

Jennifer said in something of amazement, "You'll bore a hole through the porch to run a cord through?"

"Oh, sure," Johnny said. "You can always plug up a hole with plastic wood when you're through with it."

Beany walked out to Jennifer's car with her. Jennifer paused to look at the long plank table already set up on sawhorses. Beany, still flustered, because she could imagine Jennifer comparing the upheaval in the Malone house to the ordered perfection in the Reed one, said, "We'll cover the rough planks with the tablecloths you brought."

Jennifer didn't answer. She only stood, staring about her in that thoughtful, all-seeing way of hers. Beany rattled on, "Johnny's going to have a row of the luminarias around the porch—that is, if he gets enough sacks, sand, and candles—and along the driveway, and on the grape arbor."

They walked through the open gate toward Jennifer's sports car at the curb. The big setter walked with them. He always felt it his duty to escort every visitor to the car.

Jennifer stopped and gave Beany a quiet, searching look. "Johnny's doing all this for you, isn't he, Beany? He told me you'd had a miserable couple of months, keeping boarders to make enough money to turn a room in the basement into a rumpus room like mine."

Leave it to Johnny to tell Jennifer about her rumpus room and the fiasco it was. Beany wished he hadn't— though she didn't know why. She flushed. "That's right," she admitted honestly. "Ever since we held our staff meetings at your house in your rumpus room, I've envied you having all that privacy."

An odd smile quirked at Jennifer's lips. "That's funny to hear you say that. Because I've always envied you, Beany."

Beany stared at her aghast. She stammered, "Me? My gosh, why?"

188

"Why, because you've got a house that's a place to live in, not a showplace. Can you imagine anyone boring a hole through a porch wall at *our* house? Or setting up sawhorses to dig out the grass on *our* lawn? Once, a long time ago, I brought some kids home from skating, and one of the boys dropped his shoe skates on the floor and nicked the finish. It was weeks before I heard the end of it. I never took anyone home after skating again."

"Gosh!" Beany murmured.

Jennifer went on with a wry twist of lips, "It's just that Dad can never see a house as anything except a piece of real estate. And Mother can never resist decorating the place we move into. She loves showing the house to the prospective buyers Dad is forever bringing out. I suppose it's sort of a challenge to them to see how many more thousands they can get for a house over what they paid for it. It's the realtor blood in their veins."

"Oh," was all Beany could say. "I never thought of that." Maybe if she had known Jennifer better, instead of worshiping from a distance, she would have thought of it.

"Well, think of it," Jennifer said and her words rushed forth. "I'd love to have a dog like yours. But no, he might track up the house or leave a bone on the porch. I noticed how *used* your fireplace looks. I've never been allowed to light one in our houses. It would smoke up the tile."

"But you have your own rumpus room," Beany said.

"Yes, and even there I'm always worried for fear one of the boys will drop a cigarette or someone will spill a coke on the carpet. And now this new pink house—the paint is barely dry in it, but already Dad has two potential buyers for it. So every cushion in the house, every blade of grass, every water lily in the pool has to be just so. Nobody feels at home in Jennifer Reed's picture house—not even Jen-

189

nifer." Her voice choked, and she turned swiftly to the car.

Beany could only murmur, "Oh, golly, Jennifer," and watch her friend fumble for the ignition key.

Beany's eyes followed Jennifer's sports car until it turned onto the boulevard. And with it went all of Beany's longtime envy of Jennifer Reed. Poor Jennifer. Never able to light a fire in a fireplace. Never to have a dog underfoot. Never to feel free to say, "Come on home with me."

Now she understood those two—no, three—phone calls she had received from members of the *Hark Ye* staff. "I hear the big flingding is going to be at your house. I told Jennifer I couldn't come, but I'd like to change my mind and bring my date. That O.K.?" And she hadn't had to hesitate in answering, "Sure, it's O.K."

She was turning to go back to the hubbub in the house when a car honked loudly for attention and pulled to a stop. In it were two boys on the staff of the Harkness *Hark Ye:* Jerry, the art editor, and Claude, who was to do feature stories this coming year.

Jerry called out, "Beany, are your stepmother and dad home yet?"

"No. They'll be here sometime next week."

"Doggone!" Claude said. "We've been cooking up a hot idea for *Hark Ye*. A sort of imitation of your dad's profiles where we'll do a write-up of OH's." (An OH was an Outstanding Harknessite.)

Jerry said, "Yeh, and I wanted to ask the artist in your family—"

"Adair," Beany supplied.

"I wanted to ask her about reproducing pen and ink or brush strokes. Claude and I decided we'd lead off with a
190

profile of our beloved principal. What do you think of our big idea?"

Beany moved out of her role of chili-maker, hair-stylist, and assistant seamstress, and became editor of *Hark Ye*. "It's a swell idea," she said. "Front page stuff. That way we could play up everyone who's outstanding in his own field."

"We were hoping we could talk shop to Adair and Martie Malone at the party tomorrow. But they'll be home in time for our first meeting, huh?"

"You mean you'd like Dad and Adair to sit in on our meetings?"

Claude Metz gave a teasing laugh. "Why do you think we elected you editor-in-chief? Partly because you're not bad yourself, but partly because we wanted to have access to all the Malone brains and experience. And partly because we liked the idea of meeting at the Malone house."

The art editor put in, "My sister was on the staff when Johnny was the big wheel. She said he always kept ideas popping."

Claude leaned out of the car and gave Beany a fatherly pat on her shoulder. "I hope that isn't too much of a blow to your ego, Beany. Be seeing you tomorrow night."

And they were gone.

Beany walked slowly back to the house. She was muttering to herself aloud, "Not a blow to my ego, but to a crazy idea I had that I needed a private room to hold private meetings in."

The telephone was ringing as she stepped into the hall. Father Hugh's deep voice answered her hello. "Beany, what's all this about chairs? The housekeeper tells me Johnny called and told her he wanted some."

Beany explained that they needed extra chairs for the

serving of the chili con carne and tortillas at the party. And then her words tumbled forth, "Father Hugh, I don't want a rumpus room now. It's just as Dad says, we've already got nine rooms and every one's a rumpus room. I'm just sorry I wasted all that work and all that money for paint and the one skimpy rug and one chair."

"Bless you, Beany, I'm glad. Now how many chairs does Johnny want?"

"About twenty."

"I'll get them down to you somehow."

"Father Hugh, you won't have to take Lisa's picture to send to her Marine. He's coming to the party." She realized that she was still clutching bobby pins and the comb. "Oops, and she's waiting for me to finish her home permanent."

"Give her a good one," he advised. "Beany, by the way, when Lisa outshrinks all those durable clothes she brought out with her—"

Beany laughed. "I know. You've got a poor soul they'd just fit."

22

IT was the evening of the party, the climax of their four bustling days.

I'll grieve later about not hearing from Andy yesterday or today, Beany told herself resolutely. I won't think about it till after the party. . . .

In the kitchen, Rosellen Kern, already dressed in her fire-engine red skirt, sliced dill pickles. Dulcie had bought them at restaurant rates from the Ragged Robin.

She and Norbett had come early. "I'm just itching to get my hands on Lisa's hair," Dulcie had said. And the result of her itching fingers was a wavy pony tail at the back of Lisa's head.

Lisa's skin glowed. Her lavender-blue eyes were bright. Beany could scarcely believe that this girl—not slender yet, but not fat—in her white blouse and purple skirt, weighted with gold braid, was the same girl she had first seen in front of Mrs. Fletcher's house that June twilight.

Those gold sandals worked their own magic. From the minute Lisa put them on, her walk changed. It was not the heavy, listless tread Beany had noted that first night. Now Lisa walked in bouncy rhythm to some inner melody.

This afternoon Elaine MacLeod and Ralph Tyson had driven in from Tyson. They arrived when Beany, in mussed blouse and pedal pushers, was shaking more chili powder into the two steaming kettles.

This time there was neither reproach nor misery in Elaine's big blue eyes. When Ty was upstairs packing, she clasped Beany's hands warmly, said, "Ty told me you weren't really the party-doll type, but I could hardly believe it."

Beany laughed. "Did he tell you that he only took me to the dance to make you jealous?"

"I was jealous all right," she admitted. "You were so gorgeous. Everytime I saw that orchid on your wrist, I wanted to bite it off."

"It was to cover up a burn."

Ty paid his delayed board, thanked Beany, and insisted that she come to Tyson with Johnny when he came again. They drove back to Tyson with Ty's luggage, trophies, and accordion.

Happy ending for Ty and Elaine. It hadn't been too late for them. . . . But no, Beany would wait until tomorrow to think about its being too late for her in making things right with Andy.

So much last minute scampering to put in place, to light the luminarias. The timing had to be right. If they were lighted too soon the short candles wouldn't last out the evening. Yet their radiant glow must greet the arriving guests.

194

Before Beany dressed she must set the weighted sacks along the driveway. Lisa, like an acolyte in church, followed her with a lighted candle to hold over the open tops of the bags until the candles, securely wedged in the sand in the bottom, caught in a flickering flame.

Johnny was up on the grape arbor. Mrs. Brierly, sponsor of the *Hark Ye,* had come early with her husband. He was handing the sand-filled sacks up to Johnny. Mrs. Brierly had brought flowers, and she and Miss Rutledge were filling vases with them.

Lisa and Beany straightened up from their own candle-lighting and looked toward the arbor. All the lights on it glowed in the summer dusk. Oh, pretty, pretty! So Old-World, so romantic, with the sacks like old-time parchment lanterns.

Dulcie came out of the house with the red-checked tablecloths for the trestle table. She called to Beany, "For heaven's sake, go in and get dressed."

"Just three more lanterns to go," Beany answered.

Dulcie shook a dictatorial finger at Lisa and gave her final advice, "Now remember! Play it cool. Keep him guessing."

Beany was on her knees, setting in place the last luminaria close to one of the big spruces that flanked the side entrance. Through the vine-covered fence she saw a flash of yellow taxi, which stopped in front of the house. A minute later a strange young man in a Marine uniform walked on big and irresolute feet through the wide gateway. That would be Joe Kaswell.

Beany nudged Lisa and whispered, "There he is."

For a halting moment the farm boy's eyes took in the gala setting. He shuffled his big hands as though he didn't know what to do with them. His red, rawboned face turned redder as he looked at the young folks and the older ones grouped together in the yard. Beany could sense the panic mounting in him as he stood there, fearful of walking boldly on and announcing, "Here I am."

He even took a backward look toward the gate, half turned—

A swish of skirt, a flash of gold sandals, and Lisa was running down the slope of lawn toward him, still carrying the lighted candle. "Joe, you've come—you've come." She reached out her free hand to him, and he clasped it in his big strong one.

Beany crouched close to the blue spruce and watched. The candle flickered in Lisa's hand, as she said incoherently, "When you didn't come, I was so afraid—I thought maybe you'd changed your mind—that maybe you'd gone right on to Kansas."

He looked into her upturned face with a slow smile and shook his head. "Oh shucks, no. I've been planning on this ever since I got your first letter. Then I got to thinking maybe it was pretty fresh for me to send you a telegram and say I was coming. I thought maybe you'd have another date. And then when I saw all this party—I didn't want to come horning in—"

"You're not horning in," Lisa assured him. "And I didn't have any date. I've never had a date before. I never even had a letter from a boy."

Oh yi, Beany thought, after all Dulcie's admonitions.

"Didn't you?" he answered back, his smile warming. "Neither did I. I mean one from a girl. But then I'm not the kind girls go for—if you know what I mean."

They were totally oblivious of everyone else in the yard. At last Kansas thought to blow out the candle. Now he was holding both Lisa's hands in his.

Play it cool, Dulcie had advised her. Keep him guessing. Lisa had broken every one of the rules. Well, maybe what works for some doesn't work for others. Dulcie seemed to do all right with her playing it cool, with her keeping them guessing. But Lisa's way was working wonders with a panicky farm boy from Kansas.

Beany fled into the house to dress.

Rosellen called to her from the kitchen, "The dills are all cut and ready for the party—and so am I."

Beany called back with her foot on the first stair, "Lisa's Marine is here, and it's one of those, 'I always knew there'd be someone like you.' Yes, go ahead and join the party, and tell everyone I'll be right out."

Upstairs, she made a quick change into her new blouse and the green fiesta skirt, for already she could hear the slam of car doors in front of the house, the bang of the small gate, and loud greetings. There now, lipstick, a swish of comb through Adrian's haircut, and she was running down the stairs and into the kitchen.

She glanced about its partylike clutter. She had better take some cokes out with her. She picked up two cartons.

Just as she stepped from the kitchen to the back porch, the porch light, as well as the bright light over the steps, went out. That would be Johnny, tinkering with his extension cords.

She was groping for the door knob when someone rapped on the porch door. She tucked one carton of cokes under her arm and opened it. She could see only a masculine outline against the muted light from the luminarias. It was someone in uniform. It looked like a Marine uniform.

"Are you the lady of the house?" he asked, doffing his overseas cap.

She gave a strangled, joyous scream. "Andy! Where did you come from? Why, I never dreamed—"

He pretended not to hear her. "I'm looking for Beany Malone, a freckle-faced knucklehead I used to know, with braids."

She couldn't answer that. She could only breathe out, "I thought when you didn't write—I thought maybe you never wanted to see me again."

"I had things to say, and things to do, I couldn't put in a letter," he answered. "I got yours Tuesday and I started begging for a leave right away. But I had to sweat it out. I didn't get the C.O.'s signature till noon today."

He reached out his arms and swung her down the steps. Just then Johnny evidently made the connection so that the light on the porch, as well as the light over the back steps, flashed on. The whole yardful of folks saw Andy Kern throw his arms around Beany Malone, coke bottles and all, and kiss her soundly on her cheek.

Andy released her, grinned widely as he bowed, and announced, "Applaud, if you'd like an encore."

The wholehearted applause came—and so did an encore.

He took the cokes from her and asked, "Where's Rosellen?"

"Just look for a bright red skirt," she told him.

Johnny's record player blared forth. Beany heard Lisa say, again breaking the rules Dulcie laid down for her, "I'm not a very good dancer, Joe. But you don't have to dance all the dances with me."

Again it only proved that rules didn't matter, for Kansas beamed down on her. "That's all right. I'm pretty bad myself. I'll probably step all over your feet."

And then Andy was back to claim Beany for the dance.

He said as they danced, "You know how much I like your cookies?"

"Yes."

"Well, that letter from you made me gladder than ten boxes of them. I had to get back. And, like I say, that sadistic old C.O. didn't make my leave legal until this noon, so I hurry-up hocked my TV set and my camera to get plane fare so as to come with Kansas."

"Way down deep," Beany admitted softly, "I hoped you would. Then when he came in alone—"

"I had to bustle over home and tell them to save a bed for Kansas and me. And tell them to leave a door unlocked. Because you and I have a late date tonight, pieface."

"A late date?"

"Yep, after this flingding breaks up, we're going to borrow somebody's car and take a ride up toward Twin Pine with a black pot, which we'll dump out of the car. How'd you like that?"

She drew a long, relieved breath. "I can't think of anything I'd like better. Talk about the Ancient Mariner and the albatross. It's in the room over the garage, under Headless Hetty."

"After tonight Headless Hetty will be minus a flare. Now relax and have fun."

"I was so scared of your dad, Andy."

"That's nothing. So am I. Everyone in the family is, except Rosellen."

They danced three dances in a row. Andy said he liked her puffball of a blouse; he liked her señorita skirt. "I like you," he added.

"Even without braids? You don't still think Beany without braids is like a hot dog without mustard?"

His smile sobered. "You're growing up, doll. So am I."

No one was so easy to dance with, so easy to talk to. Later she would be the hostess; later she would talk *Hark Ye* shop with her staff, later she would worry about whether there were enough bowls for the chili. But first she wanted to dance. How had she ever thought she could go for months and be only a landlady, thinking dollar-thoughts?

She glanced happily around her. There were Lisa and Kansas, dancing in rapt uncaringness as to whether or not they were in step to the music. Dulcie and Norbett were off to the side, drinking cokes. Beany could tell by Norbett's tight face that he was mad about something. Thank goodness, it was Dulcie who had his moods to put up with, not Beany.

Jennifer Reed was dancing with the college boy she dated. Pretty, poised Jennifer. Her fiesta skirt was no homemade affair. It was of heavy silk, splashed with red roses and green leaves that were outlined in incandescent beads, glimmering in the light. Her skirt and shawl had come from Madrid. "Lucky Jennifer," everyone at Harkness said, because of her trips, her sports car, her daytime fur coat, her evening wrap. But Beany would always remember Jennifer's, "Nobody feels at home at our house —not even Jennifer."

I'll always love you and look up to you, Beany's heart said, but I'll never envy you again.

She took time out to introduce Kansas around. She pushed Johnny away from the record player and took charge of it herself while Johnny danced and Andy visited with Rosellen on the sidelines. It was Miss Rutledge who said to her, "I can tend to that. You go on and dance with your nice young man."

Beany danced with Andy again, while her happiness settled into a comfortable warmth inside her. "Remember the rumpus room I wrote you about? I don't want it now," she told him.

"You sounded like a crazy, mixed-up kid ever to want one," he said.

The wind grew stronger. Paper napkins skimmed off the table and through the air like white birds. Dulcie was chasing them down, and she called to Beany, "Hey, do you suppose we ought to figure on eating inside? I felt a drop of rain."

Some of the dancers yelled back, "Let's wait and see," and Andy said, "Sure, we can always run for cover."

They danced on, the music coming through the wind in fitful spurts.

Beany looked at the silhouette of the large house with its windows lighted. She thought of the sterile perfection of another house she had once envied. How could she have been so foolish?

Let the wind whip up a gale; let the rain fall. If it did, willing hands would grab up the record player, the chairs, and Jennifer's tablecloths and take them inside. They could set up the trestle table in the living room to eke out the twelve that could gather round the dining table. They might spill chili on the rugs, but the rugs in the Malone house were used to having spots scrubbed out of them.

Let it blow, let it rain, the big Malone house would open its welcoming arms. It was that kind of house.

About the Author

LENORA MATTINGLY WEBER is one of this country's most beloved writers of family stories. Her home is in Denver, Colorado, and it is here that she has lived and worked most of her life.

She was born in Dawn, Missouri, but her family left there when she was twelve to homestead on the Colorado plains.

"I came up to Denver to attend high school," she says. "In my senior year I was captain of our basketball team and Al Weber, the young coach, always had to come home with me to carry the extra balls, score books, etc. So instead of going on to higher education, I married, and now have children and grandchildren—I have to stop and count to know how many.

"I have been writing for many years and, next to writing and riding, I'm happy to say, I like cooking—and there is always plenty of that to do in a family of our size."

Mrs. Weber has written many novels for girls, the best-known of which are the stories about Beany Malone. She has also written short stories for America's leading magazines: *Saturday Evening Post, Ladies Home Journal, McCall's Magazine,* and *Good Housekeeping,* and she conducts a monthly column in *Extension* magazine.

The More
The Merrier

LENORA MATTINGLY WEBER

Beany Malone and her brother Johnny were to run the house "on their own." Everyone else in the family would be away the whole summer. But that was no reason why the big, shabby house should stay empty. Boarders, Beany told herself, summer students from the University, would pay for her rumpus-room-to-be, and pay for some glamorous furniture, too. As editor of the school paper she was bound to be doing more entertaining. And the Malone house was certainly different from the polished perfection of the house belonging to last year's editor. A glamorous rumpus room was a necessity—and the boarders would provide the money for it.

But Beany didn't have the heart to charge full price to her first boarder— shy, self-conscious Lisa, who had never received a letter from a boy because she was so fat. And Beany wasn't too cross about Johnny's offer of no-profit board to Ty, either. Ty, an athlete, was tall, blond, handsome—and knew it. Beany thought perhaps he would provide the sparkle in her life that

This